As she raised  **voice that s**... **long time, e**... **said, 'It's Izzy, isn't it? Izzy West?'**

'I'm Dr Isabel West, yes,' she said stiffly, quite unable to behave naturally in the moment that had been thrust upon her. 'How are you, Ross?'

'I'm fine,' he said easily, as if they'd only parted the previous day. 'And you?'

Isabel was recovering. Don't let him see that you're floundering, she told herself. You're a busy GP, practising medicine in the place where your roots are. Who could have a string of dates if only you had the time. And, though the local talent might seem mediocre compared to the prodigal coming down the stairs, at least you won't be making a fool of yourself over *them*.

It had been seven years since Ross had gone to practise his medicine skills in whatever part of the world took his fancy, and had left a broken-hearted eighteen-year-old behind him. Now, incredibly, he was back.

Abigail Gordon loves to write about the fascinating combination of medicine and romance from her home in a Cheshire village. She is active in local affairs, and is even called upon to write the script for the annual village pantomime! Her eldest son is a hospital manager and helps with all her medical research. As part of a close-knit family, she treasures having two of her sons living close by and the third one not too far away. This also gives her the added pleasure of being able to watch her delightful grandchildren growing up.

Recent titles by the same author:

HER SURGEON BOSS
A SURGEON'S MARRIAGE WISH
THE DOCTORS' BABY BOND

COMING BACK FOR HIS BRIDE

BY
ABIGAIL GORDON

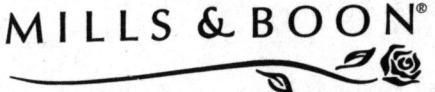

DID YOU PURCHASE THIS BOOK WITHOUT A COVER?

If you did, you should be aware it is **stolen property** as it was reported *unsold and destroyed* by a retailer. Neither the author nor the publisher has received any payment for this book.

All the characters in this book have no existence outside the imagination of the author, and have no relation whatsoever to anyone bearing the same name or names. They are not even distantly inspired by any individual known or unknown to the author, and all the incidents are pure invention.

All Rights Reserved including the right of reproduction in whole or in part in any form. This edition is published by arrangement with Harlequin Enterprises II B.V. The text of this publication or any part thereof may not be reproduced or transmitted in any form or by any means, electronic or mechanical, including photocopying, recording, storage in an information retrieval system, or otherwise, without the written permission of the publisher.

This book is sold subject to the condition that it shall not, by way of trade or otherwise, be lent, resold, hired out or otherwise circulated without the prior consent of the publisher in any form of binding or cover other than that in which it is published and without a similar condition including this condition being imposed on the subsequent purchaser.

MILLS & BOON and MILLS & BOON with the Rose Device are registered trademarks of the publisher.

First published in Great Britain 2005
Paperback edition 2006
Harlequin Mills & Boon Limited,
Eton House, 18-24 Paradise Road, Richmond, Surrey TW9 1SR

© Abigail Gordon 2005

ISBN 0 263 84705 5

Set in Times Roman 10½ on 13 pt.
03-0106-49596

Printed and bound in Spain
by Litografia Rosés, S.A., Barcelona

CHAPTER ONE

WHEN Isabel West stopped her car in front of the Riverside Tea Shop on the main street of the village she had two things in mind. The first was to check on the physical well-being of one of its owners and the second was to partake of a pot of tea and one of the tea shop's famous Eccles cakes before going back to the practice.

She'd been out since midmorning, visiting those who were too sick to make the journey down to the surgery from the isolated farms and homesteads scattered around the peaks, and it was hot and thirsty work on a weekday in the height of summer.

Often she was offered refreshment in the sprawling farm kitchens and would normally gratefully accept it, but of late there had never been time to dawdle. The pressure was on because they were a doctor short at the practice and her father, who ruled the roost there, didn't seem to be in any hurry to find a replacement.

Millie Maplin had been as well known in the village as Isabel's father. She still was, but no longer as one of its GPs. After sharing the running of the practice with Paul West for many years, she'd bought one of the new apartments lower down the village beside the river Goyt and was enjoying her retirement to the full. Which had left Isabel, junior doctor at the practice, in a situation where there just weren't enough hours in the day.

Every time she asked her father when they were going to replace Millie he hummed and hawed, which wasn't like him at all, and she ended up protesting that, much as she loved the job, she wouldn't mind some time for socialising, too.

'Be patient, Isabel,' he'd said. 'You are a natural for this job. Clever, resourceful...and kind. The village folk are tickled pink to have you back with them as their GP and I'm not asking anything of you that you aren't capable of.

'I deal with the more serious cases in the waiting room and do the most urgent home visits, so I'm not putting that burden onto you. I have the matter in hand and it will all sort itself out eventually.'

That had been last week, Isabel thought as the doorbell of the tearoom tinkled to announce her arrival, and nothing had changed so far.

Sally Templeton, a widow, and her unmarried sister, Sophie, owned the small spick-and-span establishment that attracted the many walkers who came to explore the beautiful surrounding countryside, and it was a visit to the elder of the two sisters that was Isabel's last call of the day.

Sally had been struck down with rheumatoid arthritis and Sophie was having to manage on her own until such time as her sister was able to be more mobile. But this morning it wasn't Sally or Isabel's usual pot of tea and Eccles cake that were Sophie's concerns.

As the young doctor approached the counter Sophie

hissed in a stage whisper, 'Himself is back!' And pointed upwards to where the living accommodation of the tearoom was situated above them.

"What?" Isabel questioned, not understanding either her manner or the comment.

'Himself!' Sophie repeated, with eyes rolling and finger still pointing upwards. 'Ross is back!'

'Ross!' Isabel croaked disbelievingly. 'Since when?'

'Early this morning.'

As she flopped down onto the nearest chair it was Isabel's turn to fix her eyes on the ceiling.

'I don't believe it,' she said as her voice came back. 'Why, after all this time?'

The spare, elderly woman behind the counter shrugged narrow shoulders and Isabel thought, Surely she's pleased to see her nephew back home? but Ross was closer to Sally. He was *her* son. The light of her life.

'He just turned up out of the blue,' was the reply. 'He'd had a letter from your dad and in it he'd mentioned that our Sal wasn't well, which was perhaps a good idea as she would never have told him herself.'

So he hasn't come back for *me*, Isabel thought, but, then, had she ever expected that he would.

At that moment she heard a door open up above and footsteps on the landing outside the living quarters of the tea shop. As she raised her eyes slowly a voice that she hadn't heard in a long time, except in her dreams, said, 'It's Izzy, isn't it? Izzy West?'

'I'm Dr Isabel West, yes,' she said stiffly, quite unable to behave naturally in the moment that had been thrust upon her. "How are you, Ross?"

As she fixed her gaze upon him a hot tide of colour

was creeping up her neck. Was he remembering their last meeting when she'd sobbed and begged him to take her with him? She had told him distractedly that she would love him for ever, no matter where he went, what he did.

She must have been a total embarrassment, with her schoolgirl crush so obvious, she thought as the flush deepened. No wonder Ross hadn't been able to get away quickly enough.

'I'm fine,' he said easily, as if they'd only parted the previous day. 'And you?'

Isabel was recovering. Don't let him see that you're floundering, she told herself. You're not a soppy kid now. You're a busy GP, practising medicine in the place where your roots are. Who could have a string of dates if only she had the time. And though the local talent might seem mediocre compared to the prodigal coming slowly down the stairs, at least you won't be making a fool of yourself over any of *them*.

It had been seven years since he'd gone to practise his medical skills in whatever part of the world took his fancy and had left a broken-hearted eighteen-year-old behind him. Now, incredibly, he was back, with a tan the colour of nutmeg, lines around his eyes and displaying a trimmed-down sort of physique that spoke of a vigourous lifestyle.

'Couldn't be better,' she told him breezily. 'I'm doing what I've always wanted to do. I got my degree in medicine and I'm working in the practice with my dad. I love it,' she told him, with just the slightest hint of defiance, 'but it's a bit hectic at the moment as we're a doctor short.'

'Yes. Millie Maplin has retired, hasn't she?'

'You seem to be up to date with local affairs.'

'I do get to hear the odd snippet.'

''Who from?'

'Oh, you know, *your* dad, *my* mother. He wrote and told me that she wasn't well so I decided to come and see for myself how things were.'

'And what do you think now that you've seen her?'

''I'm concerned. She's in constant pain and has lost a lot of her mobility. With regard to this place she tells me that it gets very busy and I feel that Aunt Sophie shouldn't have to cope on her own as she is doing at present. I'm amazed they haven't brought in some extra staff.'

The tearoom had been filling up while they'd been talking and Sophie, who was taking orders and serving at the same time, hadn't heard that, but she would have had something to say if she had.

The two women had worked the place up from nothing and now their home-made cakes and freshly cut sandwiches were famous along the part of the Goyt valley that encompassed the village.

'They are too hard to please,' Isabel said in a low voice. 'Assistants come and go. They haven't found the right one yet.'

'Nothing changes with my mother and aunt,' he said laughingly, 'but that's not true about you, Izzy. *You've* changed.'

'What did you expect?' she asked coolly. 'That I would have stayed in some sort of teenage time warp?'

'I didn't *expect* anything. I was merely commenting, that's all,' he told her blandly, and as if he'd decided that was enough on that subject he asked, 'Are you here to see my mother?'

'Yes,' she told him, equally happy to talk about something else. 'I call in a couple of times each week to see how she is, although she is my father's patient, as I'm sure you are aware. But Sally likes to have a chat and Sophie supplies me with tea and cake to revive me after I've finished my rounds.'

He nodded and then asked, 'Are you still living above the practice with your father, or have you branched out into a more self-sufficient lifestyle?'

What was that supposed to mean? she wondered. Was it a reminder of what she'd been like before—a hysterical adolescent?

'I live in a cottage down by the river,' she told him.

'On your own?'

'Yes, on my own.'

'Sounds a bit lonely.'

'Not at all. You're forgetting that I'm a country girl. I've got Tess, a Labrador, for company and a stray cat that I've adopted called Puss-Puss.'

'Mmm. That's original,' he remarked laughingly, and though she was still in a state of complete shock Isabel laughed with him, and thought that was how it had always been before, during the long hot summer when she'd been waiting to go to medical school and had been helping out at the surgery.

Ross had been a partner in the practice at the time and he had always been teasing her and making her laugh. Tall, lean, and dark-haired, with twinkly brown eyes, next to him the village boys hadn't stood a chance. For the first time in her life Isabel had been in love.

It had been doomed from the start. She'd realised afterwards that to Ross she'd just been a kid with a crush that he'd tried to ignore. To her father she'd been a daughter whose lifelong desire to go into medicine had been in danger of being sidetracked because her hormones had been all haywire.

Between them they'd put out the fire that had burned so brightly in her youthful heart, with Ross suddenly resigning from the practice and announcing that he was going to travel the world and her father accepting his resignation with almost indecent haste.

Unaware of undercurrents, she'd begged him to take her with him and had been devastated when he'd told her abruptly that he couldn't. That she should concentrate on her studies and forget him. Before she'd had time to get her breath he'd gone, leaving *her* broken-hearted and her father grimly satisfied.

'I'm neglecting my patient,' she told him with a tight smile as she moved towards the stairs. 'Your mother will know I'm here and will be wondering where I've got to. Bye for now, Ross.' And before he could reply she began to move.

When she got to the top of the stairs Isabel turned for a last look at the man who had just walked back into her life, and her eyes widened. Ross had found himself a clean white apron and was positioning himself behind the counter of the tea shop, with his Aunt Sophie watching open-mouthed from a distance.

'So you've seen Ross,' Sally said when Isabel appeared in the doorway of the small chintzy sitting room where Sally had spent most of her time since the onset of the rheumatoid arthritis.

'Yes. It was a surprise to find him here,' Isabel said smoothly, as if it wasn't the understatement of the year. 'Did you know he was coming home?'

The woman in the chair opposite shook her head.

'No. I didn't. It was your father's doing. He wrote and told him that old age had caught up with me and he took the first flight home.'

'You must be glad to see him, Sally,' Isabel said uncomfortably, with the feeling that maybe Ross's mother felt that she and her father had done enough interfering in her son's life.

'Of course I am,' she said staunchly, 'but I don't want Ross dashing back home on my account. I'm a long way off dying yet.'

I'd be over the moon if he'd come 'dashing' home on *my* behalf, Isabel thought, and surprised herself as she'd been sure that she was well and truly over her feelings for Ross Templeton.

'He's serving behind the counter downstairs at this moment,' she told his mother with a quick change of direction.

'Really! That sister of mine won't be able to believe her eyes. Ross working in the Riverside Tea Shop.'

'How long is he here for, Sally?'

'He tells me that he's come back to stay. Though what he's going to do with himself in a place this size I don't know.'

'He's here to stay!' Isabel repeated in slow shock as the implications of that item of news sank in.

'That's what he said earlier.'

'He'll probably commute to one of the big hospitals in Cheshire, or even as far away as Manchester,' she said, trying to adopt the tone of the casual observer.

'Yes, but where is he going to stay? This place is only big enough for Sophie and myself.'

'There's hospital accommodation.'

'Aye, I suppose so,' Sally said, 'but he says he wants to be near in case I need him.'

Isabel swallowed hard. Seeing Ross had taken away her appetite, so missing out on the pot of tea and the cake didn't matter. But the thought of seeing him all the time in the small community of which she was a vital part was turning a day that had been no different from any other into a whirlwind of emotions, and amongst them trepidation and uncertainty outweighed pleasure.

If Ross intended being around all the time from now on, how was *she* going to act? Friendly but guarded? Or maturely aloof beneath her newly acquired doctor's mantle?

However she behaved, it wasn't going to be easy when every time she saw him there would be reminders of the lovesick teenager that she'd been that other time.

'I'm not staying,' she told Sally. 'I know that Dad came to visit you yesterday, and I also know you'll want to be alone with your son...and Sally. Don't be so independent. If Ross has come home to look after you, let him.'

The invalid smiled.

'I feel better already just for seeing him.'

'Bye, Ross. Nice to see you again,' Isabel said, unconvincingly, when she went downstairs.

As he took his attention off the coffee-machine for a moment their glances held, and Isabel thought gloomily that this was how it was going to be from now on...embarrassment with a capital E.

She hoped that Ross would find himself a niche in

health care somewhere not too near the village yet near enough for him to be there for his mother if she needed him. As for where he was going to stay, there were plenty of guest houses and a smattering of hotels in the area where he would be able to find accommodation, and for the rest of it she would just have to avoid him as much as possible.

When she got back to the surgery Isabel went straight to her father's room, where he was usually to be found resting between surgeries at that time of day. It hadn't always been like that. He'd always been energetic and resourceful until the last few months, and once or twice Isabel had thought that since Millie had retired her father had slowed down instead of speeding up to fill the gap.

She knew the moment their eyes met that he had guessed why she was there, but Paul West had always been a man of few words and he was leaving it to her to speak first.

'Did you know that Ross was coming home?' she asked without preamble. 'You've been in touch with him, haven't you?'

'Yes, I knew he was coming home, and, yes, I wrote to him recently. Am I to take it that you've already met?' he asked.

'He was at Sally's when I called round. You might have warned me.'

'Why? So you could run a mile? I wanted you to meet him naturally.'

'Naturally?' she cried. 'Some hope of that when he appeared in front of me like a blast from the past. I would have thought that you would be the last one to want him back in the village after all the fuss you made the last time.'

'Maybe I'm sorry and want to make amends.'

'Don't be. I'm well and truly over all that.'

'That's good as Ross is on his way here at this very moment.'

'In that case, I'll speak to you later. I have some patients' notes to write up.'

'No. Don't go,' he said quickly. 'You need to be here when he arrives."

'I don't,' Isabel said, with the annoyance still there. 'What could he and I possibly have to say to each other? We've just done the polite "How are you? Nice to see you" scenario.'

At that moment she heard Ross's voice outside in Reception and she flung herself towards the door, ready to make a quick departure, but she wasn't fast enough. She heard him knock and then the door was opening and the next second he was there, observing them keenly and asking, 'So what do you think of the new arrangements, Izzy?'

'I was just about to explain,' Paul said as he got slowly to his feet and as Isabel watched him it dawned on her what Ross meant.

'You're coming back into the practice, aren't you?' she breathed, observing him with outraged violet eyes. 'You're going to take Millie's place.' She swivelled to face her father. 'That's why you've been biding your time instead of getting the vacancy filled. You've been negotiating in the background and neither of you thought fit to tell me.'

Her father cleared his throat.

'We had our reasons.'

'I'll bet. You no doubt thought that if I knew what was being planned I might throw a wobbly...might become a clinging vine, like I was before.'

'Izzy, let your father finish what he has to say, then you might understand,' Ross said quietly.

'I'm going to retire, Isabel,' Paul said. 'It's been on my mind ever since Millie went. I'm tired and I envy her the contentment she's found in that lovely modern apartment by the river. But I couldn't let go until I knew the practice was in safe hands, and now it will be with Ross in charge and you to back him up. I've never worked with a better doctor than him and one day you will be as good. So what more can I ask for the practice that has been my life's work?'

'I see,' Isabel said slowly. 'So that's something else you didn't think fit to tell me.'

'I was waiting until the time was right, and now that Ross has arrived it is.'

Under any other circumstances she would have been full of concern to hear that her father was giving up the reins that he'd held in his capable hands for so many years, but the way of her finding out was demeaning and hurtful. Did these two men think she was still a child?

She turned to Ross and the outrage was still there in the eyes that had been full of tears the last time he'd been on the surgery premises.

'You never mentioned any of this when we met earlier. I *can* be trusted to behave in an adult manner just as long as I'm treated as one. Thanks for letting me waffle on at the tearooms without telling me that you are going to be my boss!'

'At that time I didn't know how much your father had told you,' he said in the same quiet tones.

'Well, now you do. He's told me nothing!' And on that proclamation she emphasised her annoyance by striding past him, through Reception and out into the small garden at the back of the limestone building that was the village surgery.

As she gazed mutinously towards the wooded ridges of the peaks Isabel wished she could drive up there to lick her wounds in solitude, but afternoon surgery was due to start in ten minutes, which meant that after flouncing out she was going to have to go back and face Ross and her father again almost immediately.

A footstep on the flagged path behind her had her turning swiftly, and she found Ross observing her sombrely.

'I'm sorry you weren't told about my coming back into the practice,' he said. 'It wasn't how I wanted it to be, but your father...'

She shook her head, disbelief still strong within her, and told him coldly, 'I know what Dad is like. He doesn't take to his affairs being made public, but I don't class myself as "public".'

'I've been rushed off my feet ever since Millie left, so obviously I'm going to welcome the arrival of a new doctor in the practice, but the fact that it's going to be you, and from now on just the two of us, isn't easy to accept. I would much rather be working with a stranger instead of having the clock put back.'

'I can be a stranger, if that's what you want,' he said, without raising *his* voice, 'and as for turning the clock back, all that was a long time ago. It's forgotten as far as I'm concerned, has been for a long time. You're a woman now with a mind of her own, it would seem, so shall we call a truce? I'm leaving in a moment as I know that surgery is due to commence. Also, I want to go back and help Sophie clear up after the afternoon rush *and* I have to look for somewhere to stay as there's no room above the tea shop.'

'Why don't you ask your fellow conspirator to put you up?' she suggested coolly. 'Dad has plenty of room since I moved out.'

Ross shook his head.

'I don't think so. Your father won't want to be bothered with an unexpected guest. I'll book a room at the hotel. The Pheasant is still there, I presume.'

'Yes. Nothing has changed much since you left.'

'*You* have,' he said abruptly.

'Yes, well, it's like I said before. Did you expect to find me in some kind of teenage time warp?'

'*I'm* the one who's been suspended in time,' he told her, a flat monotone replacing his abruptness.

She observed him with puzzled violet eyes.

'I'm going, Izzy. You need time to adjust to the news that has upset you so much. I'll be in touch when you're ready to talk.'

As she watched him walk away Isabel thought that she certainly needed to adjust. Her life had been turned upside down. Ross had come back into it, and how! They were going to be meeting workwise and socially all the time.

What she had wept for all that time ago was being handed to her on a plate, but did she want that? No way. Although Ross was even more heart-stopping now than he'd been then.

She wished she could say the same for herself. Her hair was still golden blonde, her eyes the unusual shade of violet, but the face that looked back at her from the mirror wasn't going to make any man's heart beat faster, and the figure inside the neat suit that she wore for the practice was coltish rather than curvy.

'I'm sorry if I've upset you,' her father said before they began to see their patients. 'I was keen to have Ross back in the practice, but I didn't want to tell you until I knew it was settled. His return will solve quite a few things. It means that I can retire with an easy mind, Sally will be happy to have him back home, and your load will be lightened. It's been approved by the primary care trust so that side of it is sorted.'

'All of which sounds very cosy,' Isabel said tightly, 'but did you stop to think how I might feel after the way I behaved when he said he was leaving all those years ago? I cringe when I think about it.'

She could have gone on to say, I had no one to turn to for comfort. I needed my mother and she wasn't there. All *you* cared about was my career, and Ross's only concern was to get as far away from me as possible. But she didn't.

Her father cleared his throat. 'That's all in the past. Maybe I handled it wrong. But this is a time of new beginnings for all of us and I hope that you're going to be sensible about it.'

'Do I have a choice?'

'You'll be happy enough once it's happened,' he said, not giving a direct answer, and before she could reply to that he went to the door and called in his first patient, which left no further room for immediate discussion.

* * *

'I believe that Ross Templeton is here to see his mother,' Isabel's first patient of the afternoon said as she seated herself.

Jess Hudson owned the post office and general store that was the focal point of the village and could be relied upon to be first with any news—but not this time, Isabel thought bleakly.

The postmistress might have seen Ross, but she didn't as yet know that he was going to take her father's place in the practice and that Paul was about to retire.

'Yes,' she said noncommittally and followed it up with, 'What can I do for you, Jess?'

'It's my face,' the chubby fifty-year-old said. 'It began to swell a couple of days ago and now it's spreading down my neck and onto my shoulder.'

'Hmm, I can see that,' Isabel told her. 'Is it painful?'

'No. not really. Just feels a bit funny, that's all.'

As Isabel felt Jess's neck it was clear that her glands were up, but she didn't think that was responsible for the swelling.

'I can't be sure at this stage,' she told her patient, 'but I think you might have a blocked saliva duct. I'm going to put you on a course of antibiotics and we'll see what that does. If they don't clear whatever is causing the swelling we will have to pursue it further by sending you for X-rays.'

The postmistress nodded.

"I thought it might be something like that. Just as long as it isn't mumps. Though I'm past having to worry about my fertility.'

'It's the men and the boys who have to be concerned about that,' Isabel told her, and Jess smiled.

'Yes. I know. I was joking.'

She got to her feet and when she reached the doorway she turned and said, 'I'm told that Sophie is going to organise a welcome-home party for Ross and that all the village is invited. I take it that you'll be going.'

'I doubt it,' Isabel told her. 'Since Millie left us I've had very little time for socialising.' Yet almost before the words were out she was telling herself that it would look strange if she wasn't there. Ross might think she was trying to avoid him, and he would be right. Yet what chance would there be of that when he took over the practice? Once again her anger began to spark at the way her father had kept her in the dark.

They'd never been close. In the days when her mother had been alive he'd been a different man. Gillian West had been a warm, bubbly woman, adored by her husband and small daughter, and when she'd died suddenly from an embolism Paul had withdrawn into a morose shell and left the bewildered small girl mostly in the care of a housekeeper.

It had only been when Isabel had announced in her teens that she wanted to become a doctor that he'd seemed to become aware of her existence and things had changed.

Her father had liked the idea of a family practice, father and daughter working together, and had suddenly become interested in her every movement. Yet he hadn't latched onto her blossoming feelings for his partner, Ross Templeton, until Isabel had fallen head over heels in love with him and Paul had visualised all his hopes and schemes coming to nothing.

When Isabel had seen her last patient off the premises she went to seek out her father again, but his room was empty. His car no longer parked outside and she knew he would be on his way to Millie's, where she would have a sherry waiting for him and a meal ready to serve.

Why those two had never got married she didn't know. Maybe it was because they'd already had one failed romance connected with the surgery, and with cheeks burning at the memory Isabel went to greet those that were waiting for *her* homecoming—the patient Labrador, Tess, and the sleek, preening Puss-Puss.

CHAPTER TWO

A GREY heron, standing amongst rushes by the riverbank, was enjoying a tasty snack of fish when Isabel took a sun lounger into the cottage's small back garden after *her* evening meal.

Suddenly the tensions of the day didn't seem as daunting. She loved the river and the creatures that lived in and beside it, like the long-legged heron by the opposite bank, with its bright yellow beak rarely coming out of the water without a struggling fish in its grasp, and the vivid-breasted kingfishers that appeared from time to time.

The cottage was small and far from luxurious, but she didn't mind. She'd chosen it for its position and tonight, with Tess curled up contentedly beside her and Puss-Puss licking her paws beneath what was still a hot sun for the time of day, she would have been content if it hadn't been for the thought of what the future held.

Maybe she was making too big a thing of Ross's return, she thought, closing her eyes against the sun's glare. He probably hadn't given her a thought since the moment he'd packed his bags and left all that time ago.

It hadn't been like that for her, though. She'd cried

at night when no one else had been able to hear and had spent the days moping around the surgery, supposedly helping out.

By the end of her first year at medical school she'd become resigned to never seeing Ross again and had started to enjoy herself, but there had been no romances, just the odd flirtation now and again, which sometimes made her think that her fixation for Ross when she had been eighteen had spoilt her for any other relationship. It was a fact that she'd never met anyone who could match him when it came to looks and personality, but she could cope with that now. She was older, more mature, and though the looks were just as mesmerising as ever, the personality, from what little she'd seen of him so far, seemed to have been damped down somewhat.

Whether it was intended for her benefit, as a warning to stay at a distance, or that the life he'd lived during the last seven years had taken away some of the easy charm that had captured her heart, she didn't know. But he need have no worries on that score. She was over it. The mad obsession had burned itself out long ago.

A shadow fell across her, shutting out the brightness of the sun, and when she opened her eyes he was there, standing by the wicket gate that led down to the riverbank.

'Ross!' she exclaimed, struggling to a sitting position as the familiar red tide began to rise on her cheeks.

'Can I come in?' he asked as his glance took in the small flower-filled garden behind the dry stone wall.

'Yes, of course.'

Isabel was on her feet now, thinking that she'd seen enough of him for one day. What could he possibly want now?

'I thought I'd let you know that I'm booked in at the Pheasant for a few days until I can get myself sorted. My mother isn't too chuffed with the idea as she'd like me to stay with her and Sophie but, as I explained to her, short of sleeping on the tea-shop counter with my head up against the coffee-machine, which wouldn't be in the best interests of hygiene, I can't think of an alternative.'

He was smiling and she found herself smiling back at the thought of the long, lean length of him on the hard counter. At the same time she was telling herself that Ross hadn't been back five minutes and already she was discovering that the charm *was* still there. Though not to the extent that she was going to tell him that *she* could suggest alternative accommodation. She had a spare room that was available. But to mention it would be an invitation for disaster and Ross would probably refuse in any case after what had happened in the past.

So she said instead, 'I'm told that the Pheasant ranks as one of the best hotels in the neighbourhood. I'm sure you'll be comfortable there.'

'Mmm. I'm sure I will,' he said smoothly, and she felt as if he'd read her mind. If that *was* the case, she hoped he wasn't tuning in to her dismay regarding what he was saying now.

'I imagine that your father will be looking for somewhere to move to in the near future, so once it's vacant I suppose I could live in the flat above the surgery. It would seem to be the logical thing to do, don't you think?'

'Yes, I suppose so,' she said with a lukewarm smile.

She wanted him to go. He'd shattered her contentment. She felt unsettled and floundering.

But it seemed as if Ross was in no hurry. He was strolling down to the water's edge and for the lack of anything better to do she followed him. As they stood side by side, looking down into the river's clear depths, he said, 'I'd forgotten how beautiful the village is.'

'Surely you've seen better places than this during the time you've been away.'

He shook his head and he wasn't looking at the river now. His glance was on her. 'The charm of a place very often depends on those that live there. Wherever I've been over recent years it has always been in my mind that this is the place where those I care about are to be found.'

'Yes, of course,' she agreed hastily. 'Sally must be very happy to have you back.'

He nodded and silence hung between them for a second. Turning back towards the cottage, Ross said, 'I'd better be off. I said I'd help Sophie with the baking for tomorrow.'

Surprised, she asked, 'In what way?'

'The famous Eccles cakes, what else? It will be just this once, I'm afraid, as from tomorrow I'll be involved with the practice.'

'So soon!' she groaned, before she could stop herself.

'Listen, Izzy,' he said levelly. 'I know you're not happy to see me again, but that's how it's going to be, I'm afraid. As long as my mother's health is cause for concern *and* the village practice still exists, I'm going to be around. If you want me to behave like the stranger you wish I was, I think I can manage that. For the rest of it, I'm here to do a job and so are you, which means that we are going to have to find some level of compatibility.'

'I don't believe I'm hearing this,' she said angrily. 'You've been away from the village for years. We've seen neither sight nor sound of you, and now you're back you're laying down the law. *I've* kept the faith. *You* are the one who strayed.'

'Strayed!' he spluttered, and pointed to Puss-Puss still sunning herself and Tess sniffing around his feet, 'You make me sound like one of your animal friends. And for your information I've been back here a few times over the years.'

'When?' she asked in amazed disbelief.

'They were just quick stopovers whenever I got the chance. Occasions when I came to see if my mother and Sophie were coping all right.'

'Timed for when I was away at college, no doubt.'

'Possibly. I didn't want to upset you.'

'You already had…big time.'

'Yes, I know. That is why I didn't want to cause you any further distress.'

'You needn't have concerned yourself. If I *had* been around when you came to visit it wouldn't have bothered me. That other time I was young, mixed-up, missing my mother and had been left with a dry stick of a father. You made me laugh. Made me forget that I was no raving beauty. But I soon got over it. You could have come back whenever you wanted with an easy mind.'

Ross was observing her consideringly and she wondered if he guessed that she was mixing the truth with lies. She hadn't soon got over her feelings for him. She'd loved him with all the wonder and excitement of first love, without stopping to consider his feelings on the matter, and had been brought down to earth like a rocket falling out of the sky when she'd discovered that he didn't feel the same.

'I wish I'd known that,' he said with an expression on his face that she couldn't fathom. 'It might have brought me back sooner.'

'You mean that you've kept away all this time because of me?'

'No. Because of *me*.'

'I don't know what you mean,' she told him uncomfortably, 'and I don't want to. Didn't you say that Sophie is expecting you to help with the baking? She won't want to be kept waiting.'

He was smiling.

'All right. I get the message. You're thinking that you've seen enough of me for one day. Well, remember this is just a breaking-in. Tomorrow I descend upon the practice and there are going to be some changes.'

'You mean that you're going to be the big new broom sweeping clean?'

He was still smiling. 'Something like that.'

'So I'll have to watch out that I don't get swept up with the rest of the aftermath of my father's long reign at the village practice.'

The smile was still there. 'No chance of that. From what I've been hearing about you from the village folk, they'll have me in the stocks if I do anything *else* to upset you.' And as she observed him with wary violet eyes he raised his hand in a brief salute and went.

Flopping back onto the sun lounger, Isabel let out a deep breath. Ross had been right about her having seen enough of him for one day, but it had been nothing compared with what the days to come would be like.

However, the adjustments weren't all going to be on her side. She was independent, dedicated, hard-working—and would also be pleasure-loving, given the chance.

But it mightn't all be gloom, she told herself. Ross coming back into the practice might give her the opportunity to liven up her life. With a younger, fitter man in charge she would have more time for pursuits of her own. Yet was there anyone that she would want to spend her free time with?

Not really. Yet even as the negative thought came into her mind there was the memory of how she'd laughed with Ross when he'd been talking about sleeping on the tea-shop counter. For a second the old rapport had been there.

She clamped the thought down firmly. He wasn't going to get to her again. She was over all that, she told herself. She was Dr Isabel West, a respected GP practising in the place she loved best on earth. The lovelorn teenager has been well and truly laid to rest.

As Puss-Puss came close and observed with her glowing eyes and Tess, not to be outdone, trotted over and put a damp nose against her bare leg, it seemed to her that relationships with animals were much less complicated than those with humans.

Apart from her mother, Ross was the only one who'd ever called her Izzy, she thought as she slid beneath the sheets later that night. Her father had always frowned upon anyone wanting to shorten her name, but Ross had taken no notice and she'd loved it, still did. Yet it had seemed strange to hear it coming from him again after so long.

'Come here, Dizzy Izzy,' he'd said sometimes, 'and see what I've got for you.'

He would open up his clenched fist and lying on his palm would be a sweet or a flower. Once, scrunched up in his hand, there'd been a fine silver chain with a pendant, her birth stone, an amethyst, at the centre of it, and when he'd fastened it around her neck, she'd felt beautiful for once instead of plain.

She'd known that her father hadn't approved of her friendship with Ross, but at eighteen and in the process of falling head over heels in love, she'd ignored his frowns and had gone headlong into what had turned out to be a disaster.

Her state of mind had affected her studies and she'd only just scraped onto the course she'd applied for to study medicine. It had made an angry Paul West see his hopes of a family practice dwindling. Even more so when Isabel had announced that she didn't want to leave the village because she couldn't bear to be separated from Ross.

Hard words had passed between the two men, with her father declaring furiously that Ross was playing around with his daughter's affections, that she was too young to know her own mind and was putting her career at risk because of him.

Ross had retaliated by telling him that he would never do anything to harm Isabel and that her interest in him was only because she was starved of affection.

That had been the beginning of a full-scale row that had ended with Ross resigning from the practice and departing almost immediately to find employment abroad.

Never dreaming that he didn't love her as much as

she loved him, Isabel begged him to take her with him and was met with a refusal that didn't include any explanation as to why he was leaving.

She wept and wailed, clinging to him on the morning of his departure as if she would never let him go. But it was to no avail. He kissed her fleetingly on the brow and gently eased himself out of her embrace. Then, grim-faced and without a backward glance, he got into his car and drove out of her life.

It had been in the height of summer as it was now, but to Isabel, lost and heart-broken, it had seemed like the dark days of winter. If she'd known that her father had been the reason for Ross's abrupt departure it would have been hard enough to cope with, but she'd thought that she had been to blame. That her love for him had been too claustrophobic, and as he hadn't returned her feelings he'd decided that he had to get away from her.

In his room at the Pheasant Hotel at the other end of the village, Ross too was going over the day's events in his mind. His main feeling was one of relief because he was over the biggest hurdle. He had met up again with Izzy, this time on a more level footing, and although she'd been shocked and hurt at not being told about the negotiations that had been going on between her father and himself, and hadn't exactly been overjoyed to hear that he was well and truly back in her life, she had been civil enough.

His mother had kept him informed of local affairs and he'd known that Izzy had got her degree and was back working in the practice with her father. It had been while he'd been debating whether to chance coming back and risking a snub that he'd received Paul West's letter informing him that he was considering retiring and asking if he would be interested in taking over the practice.

It had been cleverly put together, explaining that the elderly GP had the highest regard for him as a doctor, and reminding him that his mother wasn't well, and that it would give him the opportunity to be near her during her declining years.

It had gone on to say that Isabel, now a mature adult, was assisting him in the practice and that he felt she might welcome it being taken over by someone she knew, instead of a stranger.

Paul had been right about the 'adult' part, Ross thought as he gazed through the window of his hotel room. The sweet, sobbing teenager had been replaced with a confident young doctor who had made it clear that her father had been wrong in thinking she would prefer someone she knew to be in charge of the surgery. There was a wry smile on his face as he recalled how he'd said he would try to act like a stranger if that was what she wanted. It wouldn't be the easiest role he'd ever played.

There'd been no apology regarding the past in Paul West's letter. Over the years Ross had had plenty of time to mull over those disastrous last few days before he'd left the village, and had always come to the same conclusion—that Izzy's father had been right to consider his daughter's career more important than a teenage crush. But Paul might have allowed him to have his say, instead of making his feelings for Izzy seem as if they had bordered on the immoral.

He'd been brought up with an abundance of love and

affection in a big Cheshire town not far away, and when he'd lost his father shortly after becoming part of the village practice, his mother and her sister had bought the Riverside Tea Shop to be near him and so that they, too, could share the pleasures and privileges of living in the countryside.

Sally Templeton had asked no questions when he'd said he was leaving for pastures new. If she'd had any suspicions that it had been connected with Paul West's teenage daughter she'd kept them to herself and generously wished him well when he'd told her he was going to practise medicine abroad. And now he was back and already wondering if he'd done the right thing.

He could see the chimney of Izzy's cottage from where he was standing, and the memory of how she'd laughed with him when he'd been discussing where he was going to sleep was one of the happier moments of a day that he wasn't going to forget in a hurry.

There would be a spare room at the cottage, no doubt, but she'd suggested that he stay with her father—and could he blame her? There were some very good reasons why she was going to want to keep him at a distance and, looking around his present accommodation, he hoped that it wouldn't be too long before Paul vacated the apartment above the surgery and he could move in there.

That was a wish that was going to be granted sooner than he'd thought as when Ross arrived at the practice the next morning Paul announced that he'd bought the apartment next to Millie's and that the formalities would be completed by the end of the week, which would leave the living quarters above the surgery vacant.

If Ross was pleased to hear that, Isabel wasn't. It was something else that her father had kept from her, for one thing, and another step nearer to Ross being everywhere she turned. She hoped that it wouldn't end up with *her* leaving the village because of *him*.

She prayed that he would at least stay away from the cottage and that he would have seen enough of her by the end of each day, just as she would have seen enough of him.

And if he found that to be the case, too bad. *She* wasn't the one who'd asked him to come back to the village. It had been her father, and knowing him there would be a very good reason. Just as there must have been a good reason why he'd been so pleased to see Ross go all that time ago.

Leaving them discussing matters regarding the changeover, Isabel went to call in her first patient of the day and wasn't surprised to find that almost everyone who'd come to consult her knew that Ross was back and about to take over the practice.

'I remember him when he was here before,' a weather-beaten farmer said as she was about to take his blood pressure. 'Could never understand why he left in such a hurry. Dr Templeton was wonderful with our kids if ever they were poorly.'

'Yes, Ross was good with children,' she agreed, and tried not to think of the time when she'd had rose-coloured visions of the two of them making babies of their own.

'Your blood pressure is up a bit,' she told the farmer. 'You're still taking the bendrofluazide, I hope.'

'Aye.'

'So what's going on, then, Michael? Are you stressed about something?'

'No more than usual. We lost a calf the other day, which was a blow, but apart from that life is the same hard grind it always was.'

Isabel nodded.

She knew that some of the hill farmers were wealthy and others, like Michael Levitt, worked long hours with little capital to fall back on.

'I'd like to see you again next week,' she told him. 'It might be just a blip, but if the rise in your blood pressure persists we might have to increase your medication a little. Sometimes it just needs a tweak and then it settles down again.'

As the patients came and went, most of them people she'd known all her life, it was a strange feeling to know that Ross was only feet away, getting to know the receptionists and the two practice nurses and familiarising himself with the routine of the place, while she and her father dealt with those in the waiting room.

Sandra Scott, a middle-aged widow and one of the receptionists, brought her a coffee in the middle of the morning and said with heightened colour, 'I didn't know we were being taken over by Sally Templeton's son.'

Isabel flashed her a quick smile. 'It is rather sudden, I agree.'

'How do *you* feel about it?' the receptionist asked. 'Your father going and this guy appearing out of the blue. We're all stunned.'

'He'll be fine,' Isabel told her, having no intention of making her own misgivings public. The last thing she needed was to see a drop in staff morale. 'Ross is a brilliant doctor and has worked here before, don't forget. My father is tired and ready to hang up his stethoscope. If we all back him up, Ross will be the best thing that has happened to the practice in ages.'

He might not be the best thing that had happened to *her*, but what she'd said about the practice was true. He was the new life blood it had been needing.

When she came out of her room at the end of morning surgery he was standing in front of the reception area, gazing around him thoughtfully, but when she appeared his glance moved to where she was standing, solemn-faced, in the doorway.

'Is everything all right, Izzy?' he asked. 'No problems?'

'I can't believe you're asking *that*,' she said in a low voice. 'Yesterday *you* turned up out of the blue. Then my dad announced that he's retiring, and, if that isn't enough, today he calmly announces that he's bought the apartment next to Millie's and hopes to be out of this place in a matter of days. And you stand there and ask me if everything is all right.'

'Yes. It *was* a stupid question,' he agreed, 'but do remember that all the secrecy was not of my doing. I didn't know that your father wasn't keeping you informed and with regard to him buying one of the apartments, I was as much in the dark as you about that. Though I have to say that for my part it's good news.

'He tells me that he's leaving all the furniture, so I'll be able to move in the moment he's gone, which will mean I have my finger much more on the pulse than it would be if I had to stay in the hotel for any length of time.'

He was looking around him.

'The first thing, I think, is to have this place redecorated and some new seating.'

She nodded and told him, 'I couldn't agree more. A grey carpet and blue walls, with cold metal seats for those waiting to be seen by the doctor, do nothing to help the patients relax. I've said it often but my dad didn't want to know. He lacks vision.'

'So how about you and I getting our heads together and working out a new colour scheme?' he suggested.

'Oh, yes!' she breathed, her grievances put to one side for the moment. 'I'd love that. Sunshine yellow and pale creams with upholstered seats to match, and maybe a deep honey-coloured carpet that wouldn't show soiling too much.'

He smiled at her enthusiasm.

'Agreed. Can I come round to your place one night and we'll work out what we're going to do?'

'Yes,' she said immediately, before she'd had time to remind herself that Ross at the practice was going to be enough without cosy little chats at the cottage.

So with a quick about-turn she said, 'Though don't you think it would be better if we discussed it here on the premises, instead of trying to visualise how it would look in the mind's eye?'

'Yes, I suppose you're right,' he said easily. 'How about tomorrow night? It will be a relief to get out of my hotel room for a while.'

He'd said it casually enough, but she wondered if he was reminding her that she hadn't been exactly hospitable the previous day when they'd been discussing where he was going to stay. Yet Ross must have known for some time that he was coming back to the village. He should have had it already sorted.

'Yes, tomorrow night will be fine,' she told him. 'Shall I get some colour charts from Tom Pearson, who does most of the decorating around here?'

'Yes, as long as he does a good job, and a fast one, too, as it will be a bit chaotic with patients coming and going all the time it's being done.'

'Ask him to work through the night and leave the daytimes clear.'

He was smiling again.

'Good thinking. I can see that you're going to be one step ahead of me in all this.'

He was happy to see that she was mellowing but was about to discover it had been fleeting when she said tartly, 'It will make a change after the way I've been kept in the dark about everything else.'

With a toss of her hair she left him to think about that and went out to start her house calls, telling herself that meeting Ross after hours at the surgery was hardly keeping him at a distance, but if she could have a say in changing the dismal decor she wasn't going to pass the opportunity by.

As he watched her drive off Ross was satisfied with the result of the conversation they'd just had. He was ignoring the tart comment at the end of it as he saw Isabel's point of view, but Paul had always been a law unto himself. He had practically ordered him to leave the practice all that time ago and under normal circumstances he would have told him to go to hell, that he'd done no wrong.

But there had been Izzy, young and vulnerable. He

hadn't been able to stand the thought of her feelings for him being turned into the sleazy thing that her father had made it out to be, and so he'd gone, never intending to come back permanently—until he'd received the letter.

When he'd read it he'd known just how much he'd wanted to return to the village, how much he'd kept the yearning clamped down at the back of his mind, and now the last person he'd ever expected to hear from had offered what had seemed like an olive branch. Though, knowing the wily old martinet who'd sent it, it was more likely that Paul would be using him for his own ends.

It was true when he'd told Izzy that he had been back to the village from time to time, and she'd been right when she'd guessed that his visits had coincided with her absences. He'd had no wish for a repeat of the blazing rows he'd had with her father and hadn't wanted to upset Izzy if she'd still had feelings for him.

But the letter had changed all that. For one thing, if his mother wasn't well he wanted to be where he could take care of her, and at the same time give what help he could to his Aunt Sophie, who had been surprised the day before at the way he'd mastered the art of making puff pastry. She wasn't one for dishing out praise, but she'd had to give him a pat on the back when the Eccles cakes had come out of the oven.

'Why *have* you come back?' she asked as she was lifting them off the baking stray onto a cooler. 'Is it because of your mother, the practice or young Isabel? She was the reason you left, wasn't she?'

'Yes, she was,' he admitted as he took off the baker's apron he'd been wearing. 'I imagine most people knew that. But Izzy is grown up now, so there's no problem.'

He left it at that without answering her question and was relieved that she hadn't persisted. He *had* come back to be with his mother *and* he wanted the practice. Isabel was another matter. He'd just wanted to see for himself that she was all right. That what had happened all that time ago hadn't blighted her life. And he'd soon discovered that it hadn't.

It would seem that she was well over her crush on him. The lonely, emotional teenager was now a cool, independent example of modern womanhood, who hadn't hesitated to express her views on the secrecy during the changeover negotiations, and had been very wary of him the night before on the riverbank. She wouldn't be throwing herself into his arms this time around.

CHAPTER THREE

Ross had asked Paul if he could inspect the apartment above the surgery and had purposely waited until Izzy and her father were on their rounds before he did so. He didn't want her around while he was viewing the place where he'd often found her bored and lonely all that time ago and had gone out of his way to brighten up her life.

She'd assured him the previous day that what had happened then was water under the bridge as far as she was concerned. An apt description, as they'd been standing by the riverbank at the time, with the old stone bridge that was central to the village only yards away. But she hadn't met his glance. Those startling violet eyes of hers hadn't been looking into his...

As he climbed the steep flight of stairs Ross was thinking that it had been a dismal place when he'd been part of the practice previously, with heavy, ugly furniture and dated décor, and he wasn't expecting it to be much different now.

When he pushed back the door and stepped into a drab hallway he groaned. He hadn't been wrong in his assumption. Its only concession to comfort was that it was clean. The surgery wasn't the only part of the premises that was going to need revamping, he decided, but this place would have to wait. Brighter surroundings for the patients must come first.

It wasn't surprising that Izzy had moved into a place of her own after living in this place for so long, he thought, and wondered what the inside of the cottage was like, as he hadn't been invited in the night before. All that they'd had to say to each other had taken place on the riverbank.

When he heard light footsteps coming up the stairs he knew it wasn't Paul's measured tread, and when Isabel appeared in the doorway Ross wondered why she was back so soon.

'I forgot something,' she told him in answer to his questioning look. 'When I asked where you were, the receptionists said that you were looking over your palatial new home, so I thought I'd pop up to see what the verdict is.'

He smiled. She looked fresh and businesslike amongst the dismal clutter. 'How about "ghastly" for starters?' he suggested whimsically.

Isabel looked around her.

'Seems a bit mild for this place,' she said with a grimace. 'How about claustrophobic? Medieval? Monstrous? My father will be dazzled by the glare of a bright new apartment after living here for so long.'

'After the place I had in Holland, this is going to seem like something out of the Dark Ages,' he said wryly.

There was nothing evasive about her glance now. She was looking him straight in the eye and asking, 'So why did you come back? You could have refused my father's offer.'

He didn't reply immediately and as silence hung between them Isabel found that she was holding her breath. Yet his answer, when it came, was to be expected. 'I do have a sick mother, in case you've forgotten,' he said, his smile gone.

She nodded quickly.

'Yes, of course. Having you back will have given Sally a new lease of life.'

'I must admit that it's good to have *somebody* who is glad to see me, as *you* weren't exactly welcoming.'

'Why? Was I supposed to be?' she asked, her voice rising. 'Not only are you here to remind me of one of the most embarrassing times of my life, but I've been excluded from the negotiations about you taking over the practice, and so was not given the opportunity to express an opinion. If you expect me to be pleased about that, Ross, you are very much mistaken.'

'How many times do I have to tell you that I didn't know your father wasn't keeping you informed?' he said levelly. 'Although, knowing him, it doesn't surprise me. And as for what happened long ago, from what you told me last night it sounded as if you were over it almost before I'd boarded the flight out of Manchester Airport.'

How little he knew the truth of that, Isabel thought, but it was what she'd given him to understand, so what could she expect? But like a dog with a bone, she wasn't letting go yet.

'What was in the letter that my father sent to you when he asked if you wanted the practice?'

'Just that really. That he wanted it to be in safe hands and was I interested? He also used my mother's illness as a carrot to dangle in front of me.'

He didn't tell her that it had contained no apologies for the accusations her father had made against him. It had been in this very room that Paul had bellowed, 'I want you out of here. I'll report you on grounds which could lead to you being struck off if you don't leave Isabel alone. All she can think of is you! Her studies are suffering to the extent that she's never going to make a doctor at this rate, and *you* are to blame for that. For distracting her and playing on her emotions all the time.'

He'd gone on to say grittily, 'You are the type that women will always be attracted to. You could have any woman you want, so why work so hard to make my plain teenage daughter fall in love with you?'

If Paul had been angry, so had he.

'Your "plain" teenage daughter has got a crush on me, that's all,' he'd said in cold rage. 'And why? It's because I'm the only person who takes any notice of her. Who cares about her loneliness. I make her laugh. Reassure her when she feels that nobody cares. All functions that should be yours. But you're so wrapped up in mourning that dead wife of yours, you've never given your daughter a chance. Maybe if Isabel had inherited her mother's looks you might have thought more of her, but one day, when you can rise above your own miseries, take a good look at your daughter. Beauty comes in different guises.' On that note he'd slammed down the stairs and immediately set in motion the wheels of his departure.

He'd been appalled at Isabel's distress when she'd discovered that he was leaving the practice, and had been tempted to find himself a new slot close by, but common sense had said that wouldn't solve anything.

That she would seek him out and it would lead to further heartbreak for her.

In the turmoil around him he hadn't stopped to analyse his own feelings. All he'd been able to think of had been not to cause any more grief for the lonely girl at the village practice.

When she'd begged him to stay, or take her with him, he had almost weakened because he'd been so devastated at the extent of her distress, but Paul's words had kept coming back to haunt him. He'd said that Isabel had wanted to study medicine until she'd become infatuated with him. That if he stayed in the village she wouldn't be able to concentrate on her studies as she should and would one day live to bitterly regret it.

Ross was able to see the reasoning behind that and if he stayed he would persuade her to get her mind fixed once more on a degree in medicine. But it was the fact that her father was making their friendship seem sordid that made him see red. As if he were a streetwise doctor taking advantage of the emotions of an eighteen-year-old girl to pander to his own ego.

As the years went by he never forgot those horrendous moments when he'd been leaving. Having to put Isabel away from him so abruptly in case he weakened as she sobbed in his arms, and then having to drive off to he knew not where.

His mother kept him informed about her from time to time. First of all with the news that she had gone to college, albeit unwillingly, and that eventually she'd begun to look more cheerful when she came home on vacations.

Much later, bulletins contained the news that Isabel

was back to stay, working as a junior doctor in the practice, and for the first time it made his sacrifice seem worthwhile.

She wasn't married, or even dating, his mother told him, and receiving those two heartening snippets of information was the start of him wanting to go back to see for himself what sort of a woman Izzy had turned out to be. Before he had the chance to act, her father's letter arrived and it seemed as if the fates were taking a hand.

And now he was back in Cheshire, had seen Izzy again, and the change in her was incredible. She was still no raving beauty, but her hair and eyes had always made up for a face that had a wide mouth and a snub nose, and as for the rest of her, the coltish slenderness of her teens was still there, with one or two added curves.

But it wasn't the physical changes that had him bemused. They were almost how he would have expected them to be. It was the change in her personality that was gripping him.

Her father had referred to her in his letter as a mature adult. In other words he'd been telling him there would be no repeat of what had happened before. So he reckoned that the old martinet must have felt it was now safe to entice him back to the village.

'I have to go or I'll be late for afternoon surgery,' Isabel said, breaking into his thoughts. 'My first visit is to the Arrowsmiths at Tor Farm on the tops. Do you remember them?'

'Yes, I do. Weren't they the ones who had the foot-and-mouth scare a couple of years back and it turned out to be a false alarm? I remember my mother telling me about it at the time. What's wrong now?'

'I won't know until I get there,' she told him. 'They have a daughter, Kate. She was in my class at junior school and later took a degree in farm management. Her mother rang earlier to say that she has had some kind of fit in the milking shed and was nearly trampled on by the cow she was dealing with.'

To her dismay he said, 'I'll come along for the ride. You have no idea how much I've missed the peaks while I've been living in Holland. It's so flat.'

Isabel eyed him curiously.

'If you were so homesick, why didn't you come back sooner?'

'Would you have wanted me to?'

'No,' she told him, experimenting with the truth again.

'So there's your answer,' he said smoothly. 'And now shall we get moving? I'm not intending getting into the thick of things until next week, when your father goes, but it will do me no harm to get the feel of a country practice again in comparison to the clinic I've been involved in recently.'

The last thing she wanted was Ross breathing down her neck while she was examining Kate Arrowsmith, Isabel thought, and neither did she want to be closeted in the car with him so soon after his return. She felt there were things being left unsaid but didn't know what they were.

'Are you sure that you're not coming along to check up on me?' she asked tightly. 'To see how competent I am?'

'No, I'm not. If that were the case I would tell you. I merely want to have a change of scene for a short time. Do you mind?'

'No. Why should I?' she replied, and led the way to

the secondhand racing green Mini Cooper that came second on her list of most prized possessions, the cottage taking first place.

When they went into the low-ceilinged sitting room of Tor Farm, Isabel's reluctance to have Ross with her changed to relief. Kate Arrowsmith was thrashing around convulsively, still, it would seem, in the throes of the fit that her mother had described.

'How long have you been like this?' she asked the stricken woman as Ross looked on gravely.

When she tried to reply, all that came out was a slurred jumble of words and her mother informed them distractedly that she'd been like that for over an hour.

'Kate hasn't been well over the last few weeks,' she told them as Isabel examined her daughter. 'Nausea, vomiting, headaches and weakness of the muscles, but every time I suggested she call in at the surgery she said she was too busy. But this morning she collapsed in the milking shed and her father and I had to carry her back inside. Do you think it is an epileptic fit?'

'It might be,' Isabel told her, after having checked Kate's heart and blood pressure and looked into her eyes with a small torch, 'but epileptic fits don't usually last this long.'

She glanced across at Ross, who so far hadn't interfered, and asked, 'Do you think it might be some kind of chorea? Kate's blood pressure is high, her heartbeat faster than it should be…and with the convulsions, too?'

'Yes, it is possible,' he replied. 'I suggest we call an ambulance and get her admitted to hospital as quickly as possible.'

Even as he was speaking Ross was putting out a call to the emergency services on his mobile phone, and once the message had been received he answered the plea in the writhing woman's eyes and told her gently, 'At this stage we don't know what is wrong with you, Kate. I don't think it is epilepsy and neither does Dr West. But until tests have been done it is impossible to make a diagnosis. I've stressed the urgency of your condition with the emergency services and an ambulance should be here within minutes.'

She was trying to speak between the convulsions but, as before, her speech was slurred and unintelligible.

'This is how people speak when they've had a stroke, isn't it?' her mother said anxiously. 'Are you sure that isn't what it is?'

'The severity of the convulsions don't indicate a stroke,' Ross told her. 'They will have to give your daughter some strong sedation, followed by blood tests and a brain scan. The essential thing is to get her to hospital. She is far too ill for us to treat her at home.'

'Be prepared for them to ask you if she is on anything, such as hard drugs, and they will want to know if she is in the habit of bingeing on alcohol as both of those things can have peculiar side effects if overdosing occurs.'

'Kate isn't involved in anything like that,' she said tearfully. 'I would know if she was.'

At that moment her father came in. He'd been finishing the interrupted milking and asked anxiously, 'So what's up with our girl, Doctor? Kate runs the place these days and we are only too happy to take a back seat. We can't manage without her.'

Ross didn't speak and Isabel realised that he was letting her take charge again as this was her patient.

'We've sent for an ambulance, Mr Arrowsmith,' she told him. 'Kate is going to need tests and a brain scan before anyone can be sure what is wrong. It should be here any moment, and if you both want to go with her we'll lock up here. Just tell me where to leave the keys.'

'Thanks, Isabel,' he said sombrely. 'Hang onto them for the time being. I've got a spare set on me. This has turned out to be a bad day for us.'

'I know,' she said gently. 'We'll be waiting to hear what they say at the hospital.'

He managed a smile and, turning to Ross, said, 'We should have been haymaking today, Kate and myself, but it doesn't look as if that's going to materialise. Is it in your line? I remember you when you were here before. Aren't you the son of Sally Templeton from the Riverside Tea Shop?'

''Yes, I'm Ross Templeton,' he said. 'And, no, I don't know anything about haymaking, but if you're pushed I'll give it a try.'

'Me, too,' Isabel told him. 'I've done it often enough before, but it will have to be after the late surgery.'

'That would do,' the farmer agreed. 'If I'm not back by then, my farmhand will give you a ring.'

The ambulance came screeching into the farmyard at that moment and all else was put to one side as Kate and her parents were taken on board.

When Isabel had locked the place up, Ross said, 'What *did* you think was wrong with that young woman? You soon picked up on the chorea.'

'Hmm. That was because I know that most forms of chorea cause uncontrollable body movements.'

'And?'

'What?'

'If you had to make a guess?'

'Dyskinesia?'

'Impressive! Where did you get that idea from?'

She smiled. 'Not from my great fund of knowledge, I'm afraid. I've never actually been involved with anyone who had it, but there have been two programmes about it on TV recently and Kate looked just like the poor women who were featured in them. It is nasty and is usually a symptom of another underlying cause. I hope that I'm wrong for all their sakes, Kate's *and* her parents'.'

'I have had experience of a patient with dyskinesia,' he said, 'and I wouldn't wish it on my worst enemy. Until recently it's been incurable, but there is now some hope for those who have it, in the form of an operation, where electrodes are implanted into the brain to control the incessant contortions.'

Isabel nodded, 'That was in the TV programme. But let's hope that it isn't that, or anything similar. Sydenham's chorea also has that kind of effect on a patient. Though in the few cases that I've seen, as it's very rare that one comes across it these days, the speech wasn't affected. Whereas Kate's is.'

'Sydenham's chorea was known as St Vitus' dance in the old days when living conditions were poor, with damp houses, malnutrition and the rest of the discomforts that go with poverty,' said Ross. 'The name comes from a place in France where there was a spate of it amongst the inhabitants many years ago. Its underlying cause is usually Rheumatic Fever. But I'm sure you will have gone into all that in your studies and don't want a lecture from me in the middle of your rounds.'

'I *am* rather pushed for time,' she told him, still uncomfortable in his presence, 'especially if you want me to drive you back to the village.'

Ross shook his head.

'I don't. I'll walk. The exercise will do me good—and I know that you don't really want me with you.'

'I was glad to have you with me here at the farm,' she protested as the colour rose in her cheeks. 'My dad usually sifts out what he thinks will be the most serious cases and visits them himself, but he couldn't have taken note of what Kate's mother said when she rang in.

'I'm afraid that he isn't as meticulous as he was and I've been carrying a lot of the weight of the practice. I've asked countless times when he was going to replace Millie and he's fobbed me off. Little did I know that instead of filling one vacancy he was contemplating creating another.'

'And then I appeared,' he said wryly. 'The last person you wanted to see.'

When she opened her mouth to protest again he said, 'It's all right. You don't have to deny it. You have a right to be upset. Both your father and I treated you badly all that time ago and he doesn't seem to have improved much with time.'

'Did he send you away because I was neglecting my studies?'

'Something like that.'

He wasn't going to tell her that Paul had threatened to testify to the police and the GMC that he was having an affair with his daughter that had started in her early teens. While it wasn't true, he hadn't been able to bear the thought of her innocence being trampled upon.

'Things are going to change once I'm in control of

the practice,' he told her, bringing his thoughts back to the present. 'You will not be expected to do more than your fair share.'

She sighed. 'I won't say no to that. My social life of late has been virtually non-existent.'

'So you do *have* a social life?'

'Yes, of sorts…when I get the chance.'

The dark eyes in the face that she'd never forgotten were twinkling across at her as he asked, 'So you're not spoken for?'

Isabel had to laugh.

'No, kind sir,' she told him. 'I am not "spoken for". I have no suitors asking for my hand in marriage. For one thing I'm always working and for another I'm no beauty. If I had any doubts about that, the disappointment in my father's eyes when he looks at me would quickly dispel them.'

That father of hers had something to answer for, Ross thought angrily. It was a pity he hadn't had some love for the living as well as the dead.

'Don't you ever look in the mirror?'

'Not if I can help it.'

'You are crazy,' he told her chidingly. 'Some women would kill for eyes and hair like yours.'

'But not for the face that goes with them.'

'Too much beauty can scare a man.'

'So can being a doctor. They expect you to be cold and antiseptic and if you're not, to have all the birth control arrangements sorted.'

'I can't imagine either of those two things applying to *you*.'

'What?'

'You being cold *or* quick to jump into bed.'

He supposed she would be thinking that she certainly hadn't been 'cold' when he'd known her before. She'd been lovestruck and vulnerable and he'd ached for what he and her father had done to her. As for the sex side of it, he supposed that, like most of their generation, she would have done some experimenting along those lines, but not just with anyone, he hoped.

'I don't know *what* I am any more,' she said, turning away, 'but there is one thing that I *do* know.'

'And what is that?'

'I have patients waiting who are more interested in their own lives than they are in mine, and if I don't get a move on I'll be too late to sample one of the Eccles cakes that you made last night.'

Leaving him to gaze after her thoughtfully, she manoeuvred the Mini out of the farmyard and drove off into the summer morning.

He could throttle Paul, Ross was thinking. With a father like that it was a miracle that Izzy had turned out like she had. Her description of herself had been given in a matter-of-fact manner, as if she was resigned to it and wasn't losing any sleep over it. If he'd thought he was coming back to awaken Sleeping Beauty, he had another think coming.

As he walked back to the village, with the shadows of the towering peaks all around him, Ross was telling himself that he was to blame for Izzy's self-denigrating attitude. His rejection of her that day when he'd left the village to commence his long exile had made her feel unwanted and unlovely.

He hoped he was wrong, but was pretty sure he wasn't.

* * *

When Millie opened the door that night to her friend and colleague of many years' standing her first words were, 'So is the plan working?'

Paul shook his head. 'Not so far,' he replied. 'I feel that I've gone the wrong way about it. That I should have told Isabel that Ross was coming to take over the practice, instead of being so secretive about it and thrusting him back into her life like I have.

'She isn't exactly overjoyed to see him. He tells me that she would rather it had been a stranger taking over the practice than him, which makes my theory that she is still in love with him seem rather ridiculous.'

'Give Isabel time,' Millie said. 'It's seven years since Ross left the village. It must have been a complete shock for her to find that he's back again. And if that was him that I caught a glimpse of coming down off the tops at around lunchtime, he is still very much a man that any woman would look at twice.'

'Maybe,' Paul said somberly, 'but I would remind you that my daughter isn't just any woman. She's the one who begged him to take her with him when he left. Who was madly in love with him, or so she thought, and has never had a serious relationship with a man since.'

Millie had poured him his usual sherry and as she handed him the glass she patted his thinning locks and said consolingly, 'At least you are trying to make amends, even though it's been a long time coming. Just let it ride for now and give your attention to what next week has in store. In a few days' time you'll be off the medical merry-go-round and settled in Shangri La next door, where you can sit back and watch how your successor runs the practice.

'Ross has come back for two good reasons that we know of. One to take over the practice and two to be near his mother. It is possible that getting to know Isabel all over again doesn't come into it.'

The call from the farmhand at Arrowsmiths' farm didn't materialise. Instead, the farmer himself rang the surgery in the early evening as Isabel was getting ready to go home. He said that Kate was being kept in for tests and that he'd dashed home for a few hours to get the hay in with the farmhand's assistance and that she and Ross wouldn't be needed.

Isabel breathed a sigh of relief. She would have gone as promised if she'd been needed but, after a seven-year fast, having Ross at her elbow every time she moved was proving too much like a banquet of indigestible, rich food.

'How is Kate?' she asked.

'No different,' he said flatly. 'We're worried sick about her. They've hinted at what we can expect and it doesn't look good.'

When he'd gone off the line Isabel sat deep in thought. Kate's mother had said that she'd been fighting off a gastric upset. She should have asked what she'd taken for it, if anything.

Going into Reception, she took her notes down off the shelf and flipped through them to see if her father had prescribed anything for Kate over recent weeks, but there was no mention of any house call or visit to the surgery.

Ross appeared at that moment at the end of a long discussion with the local plumber and the decorator, and on observing her furrowed brow asked what was wrong.

'I've been wondering if Kate's convulsions could be due to her taking some form of medication that can have that effect,' she told him. 'But she hasn't been seen by either my father or myself in recent weeks. Unless Dad has forgotten to enter it in her notes.'

'That is good thinking,' he said slowly. 'Very good thinking. Why not ring and ask him?'

'He'll be at Millie's,' she said, and picked up the phone.

No, he hadn't seen Kate Arrowsmith in recent weeks, he said when she explained what was wrong with her, but he had treated her mother.

'What for?' Isabel asked immediately.

'Excessive vomiting and nausea over a prolonged period,' was the answer. 'In the end I sent her to hospital for tests but nothing showed up. In the report they sent to me it said that she'd been prescribed metoclopromide and I've not seen her since, so it must have done the trick.'

There was silence for a moment, then he said, 'I can see what you're getting at. It's a drug that has been known to cause brain disturbance in some people. But it wasn't prescribed for Kate. It was her mother who had the severe gastric problem.'

'Yes, but from what I can gather Kate has been suffering from something similar. Maybe the family are prone to that kind of thing. Supposing her mother had some tablets left, gave her some, and they've had an adverse effect.'

'I suppose it's possible,' he said dubiously, 'but surely—'

Isabel didn't give him time to finish. She wished him a brief goodbye and turned back to Ross who had been listening intently.

'Did you hear all that?' she asked.

He nodded. 'I got the gist of it and would say that a phone call to Mr Arrowsmith is your next priority. If he says that Kate has been taking her mother's medication you will be doing them a tremendous service as the convulsions will disappear once the metoclopromide is out of her system.'

'Wouldn't it be better if I rang the hospital?'

'Ask him first and if he can't give you a straight answer then ring the hospital. I'll be surprised if they haven't already asked if Kate has been on any medication. But some people are negligent about such things and forget what they've taken.'

There was no answer when she rang the farm and Ross said, 'He'll be out in the field, bringing the hay in. We'll have to go up there.'

'I have to feed my animals first,' she told him. 'They are used to me arriving home at a certain time and they'll fret if I don't appear.'

'OK,' he said equably. 'And when you've done that we'll go to Tor Farm.'

'And what if we're wrong?'

'It's too big a coincidence that tablets known to cause convulsions are in the house and both mother and daughter have had the same problem with sickness and nausea.'

CHAPTER FOUR

WHEN they arrived at the farm Kate's father looked down at them anxiously from the top of a truck loaded with bales of hay and asked, 'What's up now? Is our Kate worse?'

Isabel shook her head.

'Not that we know of. We've come for a different reason.'

'And what's that?' he wanted to know as he wiped the sweat from his brow.

'Your wife was ill some time ago with severe nausea and sickness, brought about by frequent migraines, wasn't she?"

'Aye, she was,' he said slowly. 'Kate has been the same, though not as bad. Headaches and upset stomachs seem to run in the family.'

'Do you know if your wife had any of her medication left, and, if she had, has your daughter been taking it? We believe the prescription was for a drug called metoclopromide.'

Light was beginning to dawn.

'Yes, I do believe she has. Her mother said that the

medicine had done the trick for her and Kate might as well have what was left.'

'It might have cured your wife,' Ross told him levelly, 'but if she had referred to the instructions supplied with the drug she would have seen that it can cause convulsions in some cases, and it is *never*, *ever* wise to take a drug that has been prescribed for somebody else.'

'So you think it was her mother's medication that has made her like she is!' he croaked. 'That wife of mine is a thrifty soul. She would be trying to save money that a new prescription would have cost. I can't believe it! That a few doses of some drug could do that to our girl.'

'It hasn't been proved yet,' Isabel said, 'but I think that you are going to have to believe it.'

'So what happens now?' he asked.

'We notify the hospital immediately and leave it in their hands. With luck, once the metoclopromide has left her system the convulsions will stop.'

'It didn't affect the wife like that.'

'Obviously not,' Ross said gravely. 'Or she wouldn't have given it to your daughter. What some people don't seem to realize is that drugs can affect different people in different ways.'

'Phone them now,' he said to Isabel. 'The sooner the shadow hanging over Kate is removed the better.'

She eyed him questioningly.

'*Me* ring them?'

'Yes, you. You are the one who came up with a possible solution.' In a low voice for her ears only he added, 'It was clever thinking, Dizzy Izzy.'

'Don't call me that!' she muttered angrily as she reached for her mobile. 'That was *then*. This is *now*! I'm no longer your Dizzy Izzy. You think you can stroll back into my life as if it was only yesterday that you broke my heart. Well, you can't!'

As soon as the words were out she wanted to take them back. Ross would now be thinking that what had happened between them in the past was far from being 'water under the bridge', as she'd described it the day before. Why had she let him see that it still mattered?

Stephen Beamish, a youthful-sounding neurologist who was treating Kate Arrowsmith, listened carefully to what Isabel had to say and then commented, 'We were beginning to think that might be the case. The patient is unable to make herself understood and initially her mother insisted rather uncomfortably that she hadn't taken anything, but I think she is about to change her mind.'

'We have it firsthand from Kate's father, and blood tests, I'm sure, will confirm that she has been taking metoclopromide left over from a prescription of her mother's,' Isabel told him.

'That's fine, then. Thank you for letting us know. The next time I'm in your part of the world I'll buy you a drink, Dr West.'

'I'd like that,' she said, 'You'll find me at the surgery or at Goyt Cottage down by the river.'

While she'd been speaking to the hospital the farmer had been listening carefully and now he said, 'If what you're saying is right, we have a lot to thank you for, Isabel. I'll have to tell that wife of mine to be less tight with the pursestrings in future.'

She smiled, aware that Ross's face had been wiped blank while she'd told the doctor at the hospital where he could find her. She'd done it on purpose, of course, and wasn't proud of herself for being so obvious, but she was still simmering at the way he'd trotted out the pet name he'd once had for her as if nothing had changed.

'You'll have to wait and see if I'm right,' she told the farmer, 'but the doctor I've just spoken to seemed to think there was a very good chance that it is the medication that is causing the convulsions. By the time you get back to the hospital they might have some good news for you, but don't take anything for granted unless they give you the all-clear.'

As she drove back to the village Isabel was expecting Ross to say something about the way she'd flared up when he'd used his pet name for her and had then been so friendly with a strange doctor. But there was no comment forthcoming. He sat beside her in silence until the tea shop came in sight and then merely said, 'You can drop me off here. I haven't seen my mother today.'

She was fighting the urge to *make* him say something about what had happened at the farm, but she resisted. Ross had already caused her grief in a big way once in her life. She was going to have to keep telling herself that he was here to work and keep an eye on his mother. The fact that *she* happened to be still around was coincidental.

Once he was out of the car Ross bent and looked at Isabel through the open door, and as she turned to meet his glance she felt her face warm. Since his arrival they seemed to have been in each other's company non-stop. How was she going to cope if it continued to be like this, when just the mere sight of him made her blood run warm?

'I can't keep expecting you to drive me where I need to go, so I'm going to buy a car in the morning, which means that I won't be around first thing,' he said, 'and bear in mind that we're sorting out some colour schemes when the surgery is closed in the evening.'

'I haven't forgotten,' she told him. 'I don't forget anything.' Especially how much I loved you a long time ago, she thought, and wondered what Ross would say if he had to listen to *that*.

'So it would seem,' he said dryly. Leaving her to her thoughts, he moved towards the door of the tea shop with a long easy stride.

It was lunchtime the next day when Ross arrived at the practice in a new black BMW. Isabel was on the surgery forecourt, about to set off on her rounds, when he pulled in beside her.

'Very impressive,' she said. 'Both the car and the speed with which you've found what you wanted.'

'I don't beat about the bush. I've got some carpet samples in the back for you to give an opinion on,' he told her with a quirky smile that made her think he'd soon forgotten the things they'd said to each other the day before.

'What colour?' she asked.

'Various shades of honey, as you suggested.'

Isabel sighed and he observed her enquiringly. 'Does the sigh mean that you've changed your mind?'

'No. Not at all. I was just thinking how I wished my father had the same vision as you.'

'It's the generation gap. He belongs to an era when bottle green and dark brown were the in colours, or sometimes blue if they wanted to be adventurous.'

Isabel was laughing in spite of her vow not to let Ross get through her defences, and on seeing it he said, 'It's nice to know I can still make you laugh.'

He was moving them onto shifting sands again, she thought. Harking back to how they'd been before. Ross didn't realise that she'd locked all the hurt and humiliation away in her heart and had never expected to have to bring it out into the open again. And now here he was with his joking reminders.

'*And* cry,' she said evenly. Getting into the Mini, she left him to make of that what he would.

He was a fool, Ross was thinking as she drove off. He hadn't been back five minutes and he was already reminding Izzy of the past. Why couldn't he let it lie, as she seemed to have done?

That evening in the strangely silent surgery Ross was brisk and businesslike, listening intently to Isabel's suggestions and nodding his approval most of the time. The only thing they disagreed on was the colour of the carpet. She was in favour of a lighter colour of honey than he was, but had to admit that with the amount of foot traffic upon it all the time, the darker shade was the wisest choice.

'It will be lovely,' she enthused. 'I can't wait to see it. The surgery has looked drab for years. I love light, bright colours.'

'So you haven't got bottle green and brown in your cottage?'

'No way! I love that place. When I was doing it up I could please myself for the first time in my life, and I was in heaven.'

Her eyes were bright, her lips parted at the memory, and he thought that Izzy hadn't had a lot in her life to be happy about. It was a shame that she'd lost her mother so young. Her dour father had done little to ease the pain.

'Tomorrow I'll get on to the decorator and show him all the sunshine colours we've decided on,' he said decisively, 'and then order the carpet and the chairs that you've chosen.'

'Magic!' she cried. 'But you've let me do all the choosing. You haven't come up with any opinions, apart from the shade of honey for the carpet.'

'I'm easy. As long as the place is clean and bright, I don't mind.'

He wasn't going to tell her that her delight mattered more than the colours they'd chosen. He hoped that it was making up in a small way for him coming back into her life without warning.

As he was locking up Isabel said, 'Sorting out the redecoration of the surgery is the second good thing that has happened today.'

'And what was the first?' he quizzed. 'Let me guess. The news that Kate Arrowsmith's illness was due to metoclopromide and that there is already a little improvement?'

'Right first time. I'm so happy for her and her parents. They've had a terrible scare.'

'Yes. Let it be a lesson to them. Dabbling with drugs of that nature can be life-threatening. And by the way, Aunt Sophie already knew what had happened when you dropped me off at the tea shop last night.'

'How could she?' Isabel asked in amazement. 'We'd only just come from the farm.'

'Yes, but the Arrowsmiths' farmhand had got there before us. If you remember, he was there all agog when we were discussing the tablets with the farmer, and it would seem that he couldn't wait to let the rest of the community know what was going on.'

She was smiling. 'That's the way it is with village life. Surely you remember that from before.'

'Yes, I suppose I do. I have some news to impart myself.'

'What?'

'My mother came downstairs yesterday for the first time in weeks and was serving behind the counter for a little while. What do you think of that?'

'Wonderful!' Her eyes were sparkling. 'Your coming home has lifted her out of the doldrums.'

'It won't have reduced the rheumatoid arthritis, I'm afraid, but maybe it has made her feel more positive. I should have come home sooner, Izzy,' he said regretfully. 'It took your father of all people to give me a shove in the right direction.'

She didn't take him up on that. The events leading up to it and his arrival in the village after such a long absence were the last thing she wanted to discuss at that moment. So she just nodded briefly and said, 'It's late. I'm going. Goodnight, Ross.'

'The light is fading. I'll walk you home,' he suggested.

'No need. I'll be at the cottage within minutes, I *am* used to looking after myself and would prefer it to stay that way. There's been no one to walk me home over the last seven years and I've no wish to change it now.'

'Huh!' he tutted. 'Well, there *should* have been. What's wrong with the men in this place?'

'Nothing, as far as I know. For the biggest part of that time I wasn't here, was I? I was away at college, obeying my father's instructions to get a degree and behave myself.'

The old tartar! he thought. Sending her off into the unknown with those kinds of words ringing in her ears. Izzy had done nothing wrong. She'd just been seeking affection from the nearest source, and had been punished for it.

It wasn't just the surgery premises that were like something out of the Dark Ages. Paul's thought processes at that time must have been the same.

'What do you do in your free time?' he asked, loth to let her go.

'I clean the cottage, do the garden and go food shopping.'

'Doesn't sound very exciting for somebody of your age.'

'And at weekends I'm on call for Cave Rescue on a voluntary basis.'

'Cave Rescue! *That's* in a different league from domestic chores. How long have you been doing that?'

'Since I joined the practice. It's exciting *and* provides a service at the same time. If the paramedics who are on standby aren't available, I'm there to assist.'

'Yes,' he said thoughtfully, as another surprising facet to her character was revealed. The helpless one had become an independent woman of the world in spite of having come back to her rural roots, and wasn't that how he'd hoped to find her?

So why was he feeling so rattled to know that Izzy didn't need a man in her life, least of all him? And that she was involved in a tough and dangerous pastime into the bargain?

'And how often have you been called out so far?' he asked edgily.

'Oh, a few times. There are lots of caves in the Castleton area and once we were called out to a group of cavers trapped by floods, but that doesn't happen too often here. At Bakewell it's a different thing altogether as some of the caves there are level with the water level of the river Wye.

'We've been called out twice when someone has broken their ankle. There's a lot of rubble from rockfalls in some of the caves and it's just left there. On that sort of surface it's easy to injure the feet, particularly the ankles. In the old days when the caverns were mines the miners used to build walls with the fallen rock, which kept the floors free of debris and helped support the place where they were working, but these days the rubble gets left and makes it treacherous underfoot.'

'What does your father think about you being involved in such a dangerous pastime?'

Isabel shrugged.

'As long as his patients are being looked after and there's a nice meal waiting for him in the evenings at Millie's place, he isn't bothered about anything else.'

'So it is as well that you are the self-sufficient person that you are,' he said. 'Otherwise you would be...'

'Flapping? Floundering? I achieved my self-sufficiency the hard way, Ross, and nothing and no one is going to take it from me.'

It came over like a blunt warning, but she was smiling as she reminded him, 'I've said goodnight once and

I'm still here. I'll see you tomorrow.' And with a casual wave of the hand she disappeared into the gathering dusk.

With Tess lying peacefully on the carpet alongside her bed and Puss-Puss purring in the crook of her arm, Isabel lay sleepless in her small bedroom beneath the eaves. Before Ross's arrival back on the scene she would have been out like a light almost as soon as her head had touched the pillow after the long, busy days that had been thrust upon her since Millie's retirement, but that had changed.

Not the pressure of work. That was no different. What had changed was her ability to relax, shut her eyes and slide into sleep. Now when she went to bed, going round in her mind was what Ross had done, what he'd said, how he'd looked, all things that made oblivion hard to come by—and tonight was no exception.

He'd quizzed her about her private life while they'd been standing outside the surgery, made it clear that he thought it strange that she wasn't in any kind of relationship, and as she'd walked home she'd wondered about him. Surely he hadn't been without some kind of relationship during the time he'd been away. He was too striking to go unnoticed by women.

Maybe the next time she saw him she would ask. So far all the curiosity had been on his part. She hadn't asked him a thing about what he'd been doing while he'd been away. The shock of his reappearance had been enough to cope with, but once she'd adjusted to that she might come up with some questions of her own.

Eventually she went into a restless doze, only to be awakened when Tess jumped up and began to bark.

When she checked the time it was five o'clock, and just becoming light enough to see. She padded across to the window and peered out over the river, but all was still. Not even a leaf or a blade of grass moved. Yet something had disturbed Tess.

Her bedroom was at the back of the cottage and, still curious, she walked barefoot across the small upstairs landing to peer through the front window. As she looked down into the lane below her eyes widened. Standing stolidly on her small front lawn was a cow, big, brown and enjoying a leisurely breakfast from the fresh green grass of the turf that she'd laid when she'd moved in.

That was surprising enough, but even more unexpected was the sight of Ross, trying to persuade it to go back to where it had come from with words of quiet determination and a stick.

When she opened the window he looked up and sighed. 'I was trying to get rid of your hungry visitor without disturbing you *and* before she's eaten all your grass, but the lady's not for moving.'

'I wonder which farm she's from,' she said sleepily. 'I'm not averse to her eating a few blades of grass, but I don't want the lawn churned up with those hooves. How do *you* come to be here at this hour?'

'My mother was having a bad night and Sophie phoned me. I'd got her settled and was on my way back to the hotel when I saw the animal trotting down the road in this direction and followed it. Some farmer will be wondering where one of his cows is when he comes to start the milking.'

'The nearest farm is Michael Levitt's,' Isabel told him, still hanging out of the window, 'and he can't afford to have any of his animals lost or injured. He'll be panicking when he finds that the cow is missing.'

At that moment there was the sound of a vehicle approaching along the dirt track that led to the cottage and, sure enough, the man she'd just mentioned was behind the wheel. When he saw Isabel at the window, with Ross down below, and the cow calmly grazing beside him, he was out of the farm truck in a flash.

'I'm sorry about this, Isabel,' he said apologetically. 'I'll pay for any damage to your garden. This one has the wanderlust.'

'It's all right, Michael,' she told him. 'Don't worry about it. Just as long as no harm has come to her.'

'I'll get her back into the pasture and then come back for the truck, if that's all right with you,' he said, then turned to Ross. 'I'd heard that you were back with us, Dr Templeton. It's lucky that you were on hand to stop Patsy from going any further. Sorry to have disturbed you both.'

When the farmer had gone, with the escapee trotting along in front of him, Ross looked up to where Isabel was still at the window. He was somewhat red-faced.

'Sorry about that,' he said. 'The farmer jumping to the wrong conclusions. I suppose he can be forgiven for putting two and two together and making five after seeing you in your nightdress and me on the premises at this hour.'

'And *you* are the one who is going to tell him that he was mistaken, aren't you?' she said sweetly.

'If you say so,' he agreed blandly, 'and as it looks as if I'm not going to be invited in for an early breakfast after all my efforts, I'll be on my way. I'll see you at the practice, Izzy, and don't be late.'

'Huh!' she snorted and went back to bed, but again not to sleep. The farmer must have wondered what the situation was between her and Ross when he hadn't been back in the village for more than a few days. But after finding him in her garden at that hour, she supposed it was natural to come to the wrong conclusion.

She watched the sun come up as she snuggled beneath the sheets, and she felt a sudden surge of happiness. She'd opened doors, looked through windows a thousand times, but Ross had never been there. Yet this morning had been different. She'd looked down into her front garden and there he'd been. And for the first time since he'd come back into her life she'd been glad to see him.

Not because she was afraid of the cow. Strays were not unknown in the village. But because he'd been uppermost in her mind all the time that sleep had eluded her and then, magically, he'd been there and she'd known in that moment it was what she wanted, Ross back in her life. No matter what complications his return might bring, she was willing to endure them as long as she could see him, hear him and, if she got lucky, touch him.

It was the Saturday at the end of Ross's second week back in the village and the official day of takeover—Paul's last day at the surgery. A notice had been put up a few days previously to say that refreshments would be served during the morning for anyone wishing to send Paul on his way with their good wishes, and a steady stream of patients had been arriving almost from the moment of opening.

He still hadn't had an invitation into her cottage and was getting the message that she wasn't prepared to mix business with pleasure. That was if having him inside her own cherished little sanctum would be seen by her as pleasure. But he could wait. However long it took, there would be no comparison to that other wait of seven long years.

When the throng of well-wishers had gone, and her father with them, eager to get into his new home, Isabel and Ross began to clear up, both of them aware that from now on Ross would be on the premises permanently in the drab flat above the surgery.

Isabel also knew that the moment the decorator had completed the last brushstroke on the surgery, Ross would have him engaged on another urgently needed facelift, but in the meantime he would have to endure.

With Millie's help her father had bought new furniture for his apartment and Isabel had viewed it in continuing amazement. Was this the same man who had always preferred to save rather than spend? she kept asking herself. From where had this new zest appeared?

Yet he hadn't changed in every way. His living habits may have altered, but he was still the same secretive old autocrat that he'd always been. The way he'd offered Ross the practice without telling her was proof of that.

'So this is it, then,' Ross said as he dried the last glass. 'The die is cast. You've got me forever on your doorstep, whether you like it or not.'

'That is if I stay here.'

His hands became still. 'What is that supposed to mean? Don't tell me that me coming back to the village is going to drive you out of it.'

She had no intention of leaving the river and the rural paradise that surrounded it, and had said what she had to see how he would react. Now she was wishing that she hadn't been so flip about something so important. But instead of reassuring him, she made matters worse by saying, 'You flatter yourself if you think that you taking over the practice concerns me to *that* extent.'

'So you aren't planning on leaving?' he questioned.

'No, of course not,' she told him. 'I was here first, remember.'

'Yes, you were, which I suppose gives you sovereign rights,' he said whimsically. She glanced at him sharply, expecting to see mockery in his glance, but it was amusement rather than mockery that was there as he went on to say, 'If I remember rightly, you pointed out not so long ago that you were the one who had been "loyal" and I was the one who had "strayed". I realised then that you didn't know why I'd gone.'

'I *did* know,' she told him flatly, 'and I lived with the embarrassment of it for a long time. You went because I was becoming a nuisance, always drooling over you and wanting your attention, proclaiming that you were the love of my life.'

'And you think that's why I left,' he said slowly.

'Well, isn't it?'

He couldn't tell her that he'd gone because of what her father had been prepared to do. That would have crushed her spirit for ever.

'Yes, it *was* something like that,' he said levelly, and knew he was bringing back her hurt of long ago by letting her think he'd wanted to get away from her because she'd been an embarrassment. 'But don't start going back over the past, Izzy,' he coaxed. 'My departure gave you the chance to get back to your studies. You wouldn't be where you are now if I'd continued to be the unwelcome distraction that your father saw me as. You've achieved a lot with not much love and encouragement to back you up. For what it's worth, I'm proud of you.' And placing his arm around her shoulders, he kissed her gently on the brow.

She stiffened. 'Don't do that, Ross,' she said in a low voice, and when she looked up it was as if the years had rolled away. Gone was the calm confidence of the woman of the world. The uncertainty that a loveless upbringing had brought was there in the beautiful violet eyes raised to his, and he wanted to hold her closer and tell her that it was going to be all right. That he would never hurt her again, no matter what.

Letting his arm fall away from her shoulders, he said softly, 'I'm sorry, Izzy. It was just a kiss between friends. Because we *are* friends, aren't we?'

'I don't know what we are,' she said, gathering up her belongings. 'I never did.'

On that sombre note she went, down the stairs, through the surgery and out into the sunny afternoon, and suddenly the weekend that she'd been looking forward to stretched ahead empty and meaningless.

CHAPTER FIVE

THE first week of Ross being in charge of the practice was chaotic, with the decorators working day and night, the new chairs for the waiting room stacked outside in the corridor and the carpet fitter ready and waiting to fulfil his function almost before the paint was dry.

Any apprehension that Isabel might have felt at the thought of them working together was kept at bay as the new-look surgery appeared out of its chrysalis. To her the pungent smell of paint was like perfume, the noise and bustle of the workmen like music to her ears.

Every time Ross saw her she was smiling, and that made him smile too as he slotted himself into the running of the practice with a tactful yet determined approach. Any doubts that the staff might have had about him had quickly been dispelled as they'd got to know him. The two practice nurses and three receptionists in particular acted as if his zest was washing off on them.

One of Isabel's first patients on the Monday morning was Kate Arrowsmith, now out of hospital and free of the demoralising effects of the drug that she'd been taking.

As Isabel checked her heartbeat and blood pressure,

Kate said wryly, 'I've told my mum that if she as much as gives me an aspirin in future, I'll have it laboratory tested first. I know she thought she was acting for the best, but what the metoclopromide did to me was the most frightening thing I've ever had to cope with. It's a wonder it didn't give my dad a heart attack as these days he relies on me to run the farm. And if it *had* been a serious condition, that would have been me well and truly out of farming.

'Anyway, I'm back, and thanks for helping me, Isabel. I'm told that the dishy guy you had with you when you came to the farm was Ross Templeton, and that he's taken over the practice. I wasn't in a state to take that much notice, but when I did manage to keep still for a few seconds I knew he would be a welcome addition to the village's male population.'

Looking around her, she went on to say, 'As for this place, no disrespect to your father, but it did need a facelift and it looks as if this new guy is just the one to do it.'

'Yes, he is,' Isabel said. 'Ross has worked in the practice before but it was quite some time ago.'

'Really!' Kate exclaimed. 'I don't remember that. It must have been when I was away at agricultural college.'

'Yes, it probably was,' Isabel agreed, and changed the subject by telling her, 'You seem fine now, Kate, but I'd like to see you again in a few weeks' time. Just to make sure that you *are* back to normal. Have the hospital given you a follow-up appointment?'

'Yes. Stephen Beamish, the neurologist, wants to see me in a month's time. He's nice, but not in the same class as Ross Templeton. He said to tell you that he intends stopping by to see you the next time he's in these parts.'

'Oh, no!' Isabel groaned. 'When we spoke about the possibility of it being the metoclopromide that might be affecting you, I invited him to call if ever he was passing. It was on the spur of the moment. I wasn't really serious and now what have I let myself in for?'

'It strikes me that neither of us have time for that kind of thing,' Kate said, laughing at her dismay. 'I'm too busy mucking out and you're fully occupied with this place. But you know what they say, all work and no play makes Jill a dull girl.'

Oh, she was dull all right, Isabel thought when Kate had gone. Maybe not here at the surgery, but there wasn't much sparkle in the rest of her life. Perhaps she should buy some new clothes, but they would only improve her on the outside. It was what was inside her that needed livening up and she knew that her mind would never have been travelling along those tracks if the man in the consulting room next to hers hadn't come back.

It was the weekend again and with it had come another opportunity for Isabel to mix with folk that she'd known all her life. The week before it had been her father's farewell at the surgery. This week there was to be a welcome-home gathering for Ross at the Riverside Tea Shop with an open invitation for anyone to come.

Sophie had mentioned it during the week. 'You'll be joining us on Saturday afternoon, I hope,' she'd said, when Isabel had called in for her afternoon snack. 'We're not opening this place during the day, which will give us the time and space to get ready for a party for Ross.'

Taken aback, Isabel had remembered vaguely that Jess from the post office had mentioned something of the sort when Ross had first come back, but with so much having happened since she'd forgotten all about it.

'Yes, of course I'll be there,' she'd said, trying to show some enthusiasm with the thought uppermost that the majority of the guests would know why he'd left in the first place and would be wondering if there was anything going on between them now. The answer to that question, should it be asked, was no. There was nothing going on, or likely to be. Her passion for Ross was dead, she told herself.

So why when she'd heard about the party had her first thoughts been about what she should wear, and would she have time to have her hair washed and styled on Saturday morning after the short weekend surgery?

Second thoughts had followed quickly on the heels of the first and they'd been more in keeping with the person she saw herself as. Ross hadn't found her attractive before, and she hadn't really improved. So he wasn't likely to be bowled over by her charms this time, was he?

'Does he know what you're planning?' she'd asked Sophie.

She had shaken her head. 'No. We're telling everyone to keep quiet about it. He doesn't like fuss, but we're hoping that he will see this in the spirit that it's meant.'

'Is my father coming?'

The older woman had shrugged her narrow shoulders.

'I don't know if his conscience will let him. Although he has redeemed himself somewhat by asking Ross to take over the practice.'

Isabel had observed her questioningly.

'I'm not with you.'

'No, you're not, are you?' Sophie had replied. She'd gone to serve a customer who'd just come in and said over her shoulder, 'Perhaps it's better that way. Paul used you as a pawn to get his own way.'

As Isabel had driven home the word had kept going round in her mind. A pawn. What had Sophie meant by it? The next time she spoke to her father she would ask him if there'd been other things going on in the background when Ross had left the practice. If there had been, she'd known nothing of them. *Her* concern had been that the only person who'd ever taken any notice of her had been going out of her life, and she hadn't been able to bear it.

In the end Isabel decided to wear to the party a black silk top and white trousers that she'd had for ages. Giving the hairdresser's a miss, she washed her hair with her favourite shampoo and when it was dry she brushed it into a shining bob around the face that she'd always wished had belonged to somebody else.

The last thing she wanted was for Ross to think she'd dressed up for him, but when she arrived at the tea shop and found that Kate Arrowsmith had discarded her 'mucking-out' image and was dressed in an outfit that would have graced the catwalk during London Fashion Week she felt like turning round and going home.

There was no sign of the prodigal doctor so far. When the door opened again it was her father and Millie arriving, and immediately Sophie's comments came back to plague her. But it was not the time or the place for raking up old wrongs, she decided, and when someone said that Ross had come into view and would be arriving at any moment, she reluctantly joined the crush hiding in the back room and waited for him to appear.

'Aunt Sophie, where are you? What's going on?' he called from the bottom of the stairs, having seen the abundance of food laid out in the deserted tea shop and noted the absence of any sign of life.

It was the cue for the door of the back room to be thrown open, and as half of the population of the village came pouring out, with his mother moving painfully in the forefront, he stepped back in amazement.

'Welcome home, Ross,' she said in a choked voice.

Someone at the back of the gathering said, 'Aye, welcome to the new doctor. We remember him from before and hope that this time he's going to stay.'

Isabel watched Ross's glance go round the room until it came to rest on her, and she held her breath as she waited to hear what he would have to say. It was as if the rest of those present were receding and there was just the two of them in the old raftered building.

'I never wanted to leave the first time,' he said evenly, 'but there were circumstances that made it the wisest thing to do. This time I intend to stay. Nothing and no one will drive me away. Thank you for this warm welcome.' His glance had shifted to his mother and his aunt. 'I don't need to guess whose idea it was.'

In the pause that followed, her father stepped forward. 'Ross Templeton was hand-picked by me,' he said in the flat voice that Isabel knew so well. 'I wanted to leave the practice in safe hands and couldn't think of any that would be safer than his.'

Ross had been smiling before but now his expression closed up, and when it seemed that he wasn't going to reply to her father's vote of confidence Sophie said, 'Shall we start with a toast to the new doctor and the village practice?'

As there was a surge towards the food and drink Isabel slipped out through the back door. She was wishing she hadn't come. All those there would have known what Ross had meant when he'd said there had been circumstances that had made it wise for him to leave the village all that time ago. They were circumstances that she alone had created.

Or, at least, that was what she'd always thought, until the other day when Sophie had described her as a pawn in some game of her father's and she had wondered what she'd meant. But if that had been the case, why had he asked Ross to come back and just made that speech of recommendation?

She sighed. Life had been so uncomplicated before and now it was full of doubts and uncertainties. Neither Ross nor her father had thought to comment on the changes she was having to make in *her* life. Or how she had kept the practice going through the last few months when her father had slowed down to such an extent. It had been like the Ross-and-Paul show back there, with no mention of lesser mortals.

Where the dickens had Izzy gone? Ross wondered as his eyes scanned the room. He hoped she hadn't gone home after he'd reminded those present of what she'd been like when he'd left, instead of directing their attention to the cool young doctor in their midst.

Every time he was about to seek her out he was waylaid by someone wanting to chat and he was becoming more on edge with every passing moment. He should have been enjoying this occasion, so thoughtfully arranged by those who loved him, but he was finding it impossible to relax with his concern for Izzy uppermost in his mind. Close behind it was his annoyance at the cheek of Paul West, who was using the occasion to give himself a pat on the back for bringing about Ross's return to the village.

If he left the party to go and look for her, it would seem rude, he told himself, and it might upset his mother and Sophie, so he put a fixed smile on his face and stayed where he was.

When Izzy came striding in through the back door he gave a sigh of relief. She didn't look too happy but at least she hadn't gone home and he wished that Kate, who had attached herself to him as soon as he'd arrived, would go and talk to someone else so that he could go to Izzy.

The first thing Isabel saw when she went back to join the party was Kate still monopolising Ross, preening and posing beside him in the glamorous outfit with all the tenacity of a leech. And it didn't look as if he had any objections as he was making no effort to detach himself from the farm manager's presence, so Isabel turned to go back outside.

But this time she wasn't fast enough. Ross quickly excused himself from Kate and caught up with her as she was lifting the latch.

'Where have you been?' he asked.

'In the back garden. Why?'

'I thought you'd gone.'

'Why would you think that? And would it have mattered if I had?'

'Yes, it would. For one thing, when your father interrupted what I was saying, I was about to remind everyone in there that I wouldn't be able to cope without *you*. That you are intelligent, hard-working, reliable and—'

'Do not react to soft-soaping?'

'What do you mean?'

'I mean that you would have been singing my praises to take their minds off how you'd reminded them of what I was like when you left.'

'My comments were not meant like that at all,' he told her firmly. 'They were for your father to digest. Whether they sank in or not, I don't know, but I *am* aware of how they must have sounded to you, and I'm sorry, Izzy.'

She shrugged.

'Forget it. Ross. It's all in the past. Enjoy your party.' Leaving him still not happy, she strolled across to where Kate was now glowing up at a tall, fair-haired man in expensive casual clothes.

'Meet Stephen Beamish,' she said, when Isabel joined them.

'The neurologist!' she exclaimed.

He smiled. 'None other. I *did* say I'd look you up, didn't I?'

'Yes, you did. How did you know I was here?'

'There was no one at your cottage and a farmer who was driving past told me that you would most likely be at the welcoming party for the new GP. So I came here and was invited in, little expecting that Kate would be the first person to greet me.' His glance was on the outfit. And what a transformation from the last time he'd seen her. 'But it's you that I've come to see, Dr West, the person who solved the mystery of the metoclopromide.'

Isabel was only half listening. She was looking to where Ross was still standing by the back door where she'd left him. She didn't want to talk to this man who'd appeared out of the blue. She wanted to be with Ross, on their own, where she could ask him to explain the real reason for his dislike of her father.

It couldn't be that serious, she reasoned, or her father wouldn't have asked Ross to take over the practice. He'd spoken highly of him earlier, so why were Ross and Sophie hinting that there had been, and still were, undercurrents?

While she'd been thinking, Kate had sauntered off and gone to stand close by Ross again. Stephen Beamish said, 'I thought I'd dine somewhere near if I can find a good restaurant. It's beautiful countryside around here, isn't it?'

'Yes. It's delightful,' Isabel agreed. 'I would never want to live anywhere else.'

'And that being so, you'll know all the best restaurants.'

'Yes, more or less.'

'So how about dining with me this evening? Your choice of venue.'

She was about to refuse, but the sight of Ross and Kate engrossed in each other once more made her change her mind.

'Yes, all right,' she agreed. 'The party will be over at

about five, which will give me time to go home and change. What time would you want to eat?'

'About seven, if that's all right with you. I'll pick you up at your place, and in the meantime I'll have a look round the village. Maybe see what sort of properties are for sale.'

'So are you not married?'

'Good gracious, no! I've never had the time or met the right woman. What about you?'

'I'm single, too. Though I did once meet the right man.'

'And where is he now?'

'He's around. But I was over it a long time ago.'

'Good. So I'll see you at seven.'

She nodded. 'Yes.'

The neurologist was pleasant and smart, she thought when he'd gone, but with Ross back in her life and standing just a few feet away she was already regretting having agreed to dine with him. Yet why not? she reasoned. Her feelings for Ross were dead and buried...weren't they?

'Kate tells me that fellow is the neurologist you were talking to on the phone that day at their farm,' Ross said unsmilingly when his limpet-like admirer had gone home to do the milking.

'Yes, Stephen Beamish,' Isabel said coolly. 'He's asked me to dine with him this evening.'

Ross whistled softly. 'He doesn't let the grass grow under his feet, does he?'

'Neither does Kate Arrowsmith if it comes to that.'

'Maybe not, but she hasn't asked for a date.'

'Give her time. *And* she won't be the only one.'

'Why would that be?'

'Don't you ever look in the mirror?'

'Only to search for grey hairs or to straighten my tie. But getting back to this Beamish guy. What do you know about him?'

'Just that he's a neurologist at the hospital.'

'Exactly. How do you know that he hasn't got a wife and family?'

'He says he hasn't, because he's never found the right woman.'

'And you believe him?'

'Does it matter? Tonight is just a one-off. For all I know, *you* might have a wife and family tucked away somewhere. Seven years is a long time.'

Dark brows were rising as he said incredulously, 'A family? That I haven't told you about? I know I'm not top of your list of favourite people, but it's insulting that you could think me so devious. I could have had one. I met someone who would have been only too willing to tie the knot if I'd given her any encouragement, but guess what? She was the daughter of one of my colleagues in the Dutch clinic where I was working, and I didn't want to go down that road again.'

'And what road would that be?' she snapped, hoping that no one could hear what they were saying.

'I think you know the answer to that,' he said abruptly, with his glance on what was going on behind her, and when she turned Isabel found herself looking into her father's cold blue eyes.

'We're off,' he said. 'If either of you need me for anything you know where I am.' And on that brief note of farewell he went.

As they watched him go, with a back straight as a ramrod and only the slightest hint of stiffness in his movements, Isabel said, 'You don't like my father, do you?'

'No. I don't. I don't like him one bit because of how he has always treated you, and yet in a grudging sort of way I respect him.'

'He would have been different if I'd looked like my mother.'

'Maybe, but it does him no credit. He should love you for what you are. Millie is no oil painting, but he doesn't undermine *her* confidence like he has always done yours.'

'That is all in the past,' she told him stiffly. 'I'm my own woman now. I don't dance to his tune any more, or anyone else's for that matter, and now I'm going as I want to get ready for tonight.'

She was smarting at his easy acceptance of her lack of beauty and being put in the same category as the elderly spinster who seemed to be the only one on her father's wavelength. Maybe that was why Ross was making such a fuss about her date with Stephen Beamish. He couldn't believe that, next to Kate in the classy outfit, *she* had been the object of the other man's attention.

'Where is he taking you?'

She shrugged. 'It's my choice. Probably the Pheasant. It's as good as anywhere in the area.'

'Have a nice time, then,' he said in an easier tone.

Still ruffled, Isabel said, 'So you're not going to comment on the strangeness of the handsome neurologist asking *me* out when Kate was fluttering around like a beautiful butterfly?'

'Beauty is in the eye of the beholder,' he replied smoothly. He was looking around him. 'I think I need to spread myself around a bit. These people have come to welcome me. The least I can do is renew my acquaintance with those I knew before and introduce myself to any newcomers.'

'Yes, of course,' she said quickly. 'I won't delay you any longer. I'll see you on Monday morning at the surgery.'

You might be seeing me before that, Ross thought as Isabel made her farewells to his mother and aunt. Kate had told him that while she'd been in hospital she'd heard the staff discussing Stephen Beamish. She'd discovered that he was well known as a womaniser who liked to boast of his conquests, and the thought that he might intend to add Isabel to the list was not acceptable.

But he, Ross, had already upset her by appearing to fuss over something that was not his business *and* he had just been told that she didn't dance to anyone's tune but her own these days, so how was he going to keep Izzy safe from a guy who used women for just one thing, without upsetting her further?

Her conversation with Ross at the tea shop had put the blight on any pleasure Isabel might have felt at the prospect of dining out with an attractive man. For one thing, Ross had made her feel that she'd been just a bit too quick to agree to a date with a stranger, and for another had compared her attractions with those of a woman old enough to be her mother.

On top of that, he'd made no bones about not wanting to have anything more to do with doctors' daughters, as if she'd set the stamp on women of that ilk with her hysteria and the foolish romanticising that lay in the past like an insurmountable barrier.

If she'd dressed down for Ross's welcome-home party, she was going to dress up for tonight, she thought defiantly. The doctor from the city wasn't going to be shown up by the country bumpkin. Taking off its hanger a short black cocktail dress that hadn't seen the light of day before, she prepared to make the best of her resources.

Stephen Beamish had charm, lots of it, Isabel decided as the evening progressed, but it was a practiced sort of charm, like a script that he'd rehearsed. And he liked to touch. When he'd helped to remove her wrap after she'd seated herself in the hotel restaurant, he'd let his hands linger on her bare shoulders and his leg movements beneath the table were suspect.

If this was for starters, what was he going to be like when he took her home? she thought. He'd already said that he'd love to see the inside of her cottage and the look in his eyes told her that it wasn't the downstairs part of it that he was interested in.

In the middle of the meal she excused herself to go to the ladies' room for a respite while she gathered her thoughts. As she was making her way there, Isabel stopped in her tracks. Ross was seated at a table for one in a small alcove that was almost out of sight from the rest of the diners.

He was enjoying his meal and hadn't seen her until she planted herself in front of him and muttered angrily, 'What are *you* doing here?'

'The same as you...eating,' he said calmly. 'How's it going with the hospital stud?'

'You knew, didn't you?'

'What? That he's as fresh as a basket of whelks? Yes. Kate told me that he's after everything in skirts.'

'And that's why you're snooping on me.'

'Shall we change that to "keeping a watchful eye"? If you have no problems, I'll leave you both to it. On the other hand, if you want to make a dash for it I can come up with an urgent call from a patient or something.'

'Stephen won't believe that. Anyone in the NHS knows that night calls are dealt with by an emergency service.'

So you *do* want to get away?'

'Yes,' she admitted. 'But without being rude. I *did* let myself in for this.'

'Go back to your table and leave it to me,' he said.

She nodded, feeling that she had made a prize fool of herself, and without further conversation did as Ross had suggested.

Within minutes he appeared apologetically by her side and said to her companion, 'I'm sorry to interrupt your meal, but I felt that I had to let Izzy know that her dog, Tess, seems to have escaped from the garden and is running free down by the riverbank.'

Stephen yawned.

'Can't *you* go and catch the dog?'

'She will only answer to me,' Isabel said, getting to her feet. 'I'm sorry to have to rush off, Stephen, but I must see to my dog. My animals mean everything to me.' And before he could protest further she left the dining room at a quick pace, with Ross close behind.

When they were clear of the hotel she said, 'Go on, Ross, say it. You were right and I was wrong.'

'I'm not going to say any such thing. I should have

told you what Kate said about Beamish's reputation, but I knew how you would see that.'

'How? How would I have seen it?'

'As interference, treating you like a child. And I knew that you'd had your fill of that. Was he as he'd been described?'

'Mmm. Playing footsie and stroking my shoulders.'

'I've a good mind to go back and sort him out.'

'No, don't! The fault was mine. I'll bet you thought that I was so desperate I would go out with anyone. Though if you did, you were wrong. I *was* being childish.'

'How?'

'I was trying to make you jealous.'

'After what your father and I did to you, I have no rights where you are concerned, Izzy,' he said gravely. 'No right to be jealous. No right to interfere in your life. And if I ever hurt you again, I will never forgive myself.'

'You were the bright star in my dismal life in those days,' she said wistfully. 'Kind, funny, understanding. And I spoilt it all because I didn't know how to behave.'

They were walking along the lane that led to her cottage and he stopped and took her arm, turning her round to face him.

'*You* did nothing wrong, Izzy. You were dealing with two mature men. One of them was determined you would go to medical school come what may, and the other was so afraid of you being dragged into a scandal he took off into the unknown and left you to cope all by yourself.'

The light had gone and a yellow summer moon was shining down on them as with eyes wide and questioning she asked, 'What sort of a scandal?'

'Your father threatened that if I didn't leave the practice he would report me to the police and the General Medical Council in the hope that I would get a criminal record and be struck off for having an affair with his daughter.'

'But we...you didn't!'

'I knew that and so did you, and even if it *had* been true, you were over the age of consent. But he said he would tell them that it had been going on since your early teens.

'He always wanted you in the practice and when you refused to be separated from me he decided that you were going to medical school by fair means or foul. He didn't credit me with having the decency to persuade you to change your mind and issued the ultimatum, which gave me no choice.

'With regard to his ridiculous allegations I would have told him to go to hell and taken my chances, it would have been his word against mine. But I wasn't having your innocence dragged through the mire to prove mine, regarding something that we hadn't done, so I went.'

'How could my father do that?' she cried. 'It was wicked.'

Ross's smile was wry. 'It might have been, but it worked. He got the doctor that he wanted for the practice. He did you a favour in an underhanded sort of way, because look at you now. He *has* to be proud of you.'

'Huh! Maybe he is. But what about the way he messed up *your* life? Has he said he's sorry for that?'

'He's asked me to come back, hasn't he? Obviously he doesn't see me as a threat any more.'

He could see the moon reflected in her eyes as she said, 'So why don't we prove him wrong?'

'Like this, you mean?' he said softly as he reached out for her and took her in his arms.

'Mmm,' she murmured as she lifted her mouth to his.

And for Stephen, who had reluctantly decided that the least he could do was go and help look for the wretched dog, there seemed little else to do but turn his car round and go back to where he had come from.

CHAPTER SIX

THE sound of the car reversing noisily behind them brought the kiss to an end and Isabel out of Ross's arms.

'What's wrong?' he asked as it sped off into the night. 'Was it someone you know?'

'It looked like the car that Stephen picked me up in earlier.'

'So if he hasn't got the message now, he never will,' Ross said, unperturbed, then added more seriously with his gaze on the lips that were still warm from his kiss, 'What is more important is what sort of a message *you* were getting when we were interrupted. I wouldn't want you to get any wrong ideas.'

'Such as?' she questioned flatly, as the magic drained away.

'That I would pursue you just to get at your father, as that was what you were suggesting, wasn't it?'

'I said it on the spur of the moment as I don't think that either of us have anything to thank him for.'

'Much as I don't like the man, that isn't true,' he said levelly. 'You might never have entered the profession that you enjoy so much if it hadn't been for your father's scheming, and he *has* given me the chance to come back to the place where I've always wanted to be.'

'Look, Ross,' she said angrily. 'I can see that you're regretting what just happened between us and I suppose I can't blame you. Once bitten twice shy when it comes to the likes of me, I suppose. I've just told you that I said what I did about calling my father's bluff without thinking. I suppose in my own stupid way I was throwing out a challenge. It won't happen again. In future I will consider every word before I say it. This has been a strange evening, spent with two different men. I suppose I should consider myself lucky. Except that one of them couldn't keep his hands off me and the other forgot himself for a moment and couldn't wait to tell me how much he regretted it.

'Thanks for walking me home and rescuing me from that man. But I would have managed on my own, as I've had to do for as long as I can remember, if you hadn't shown up.'

'Have you quite finished putting me in my place?' he said calmly, when she stopped for breath.

'Yes.'

'Good. Then I'll be off, until we meet again on Monday morning, bright and early.'

'Of course,' she said abruptly, with the thought that 'early' she might be, but 'bright'? Not after tonight!

He was a fool, Ross thought as he walked home through the moonlit night. Not for rescuing Izzy from the clutches of the lecherous neurologist—he could no more have sat around and done nothing about that than fly to the moon. He was calling himself a fool because he'd done the very thing he'd promised himself he wouldn't do, let Izzy get to him.

It had been as natural as breathing to take her in his arms and kiss the mouth that was reaching up to his, and it would have gone on from there, but in a strange sort of way Stephen Beamish had got his revenge for being left in the lurch. The noise of his car reversing behind them in the lane had broken the spell and brought him to his senses.

He had only been back in the village a short time and already he was causing complications between Izzy and himself. He'd promised himself before he'd come back that he would wait, he'd had plenty of practice at doing that, and take things slowly. Yet what had happened? The opportunity had presented itself and he'd taken it.

But he had to remind himself that their working relationship was vitally important. He wanted to establish that before anything else, as all eyes would be on him, Paul West's in particular, observing just how successfully he was running the practice.

When he arrived back at the surgery he strolled around the refurbished rooms before going up to the dreary flat, and there was a smile on his face as he recalled Izzy's pleasure as she'd watched the transformation take place.

He knew he'd upset her back there in the lane. He'd thought the right thoughts but said the wrong words. It would have been so easy to let the tenderness that she'd always aroused in him take over, but he had to get it right this time. No more hurts for the girl with the beautiful violet eyes. The two of them had a practice to run in a pretty village surrounded by towering peaks and bleak moorland, and until he'd got his hands securely on the reins the dream that he held in his heart would have to stay there just a little while longer.

'My goodness!' Jess said when she arrived at the practice on Monday morning. 'What a transformation! I feel better already just for seeing some bright colours.'

'So you don't want to see the doctor, then?' one of the receptionists said laughingly.

She sighed. 'I'm afraid I do. Have you seen my face? It's still swollen. Isabel said to come back if the tablets she gave me didn't remove the swelling.'

The receptionist nodded.

'Yes. She knows you are coming. Your notes have gone in to her so take a seat and she'll call you when she's ready.'

Isabel had been glad to get to work that morning. She hadn't been able to settle anything during Sunday, the memory of what had happened in the lane on Saturday night between Ross and herself uppermost in her mind.

When he'd taken her in his arms she'd been ready to let the sudden unexpected chemistry take over, seeing it as just a romantic moment in the moonlight between friends, but she'd been amazed by how right it had felt. It had been like coming home after a long journey and his kiss had set the seal on it.

Bemused, she'd wanted more and had been desolate when the car behind them had broken the spell. But it had been clear that Ross hadn't seen it in the way she had. He'd been straight onto the defensive, warning her off. Could she blame him? She'd already been responsible for a big blip in his career once, so he wasn't going to let it happen again.

From now on she was going to be a doctor first and foremost, she'd told herself during a sleepless night, and the woman who longed for love and affection was going to keep a low profile.

'Everything all right?' Ross had questioned warily when she'd arrived at the surgery that morning.

'Yes, fine,' she'd replied breezily, with the vow she'd made in the dark hours of the previous night at the front of her mind.

'Good, as we appear to have a full waiting room,' he told her. 'And by the way, if you hear any noises coming from up above I'm having a new kitchen and bathroom fitted, starting today.'

'That's quick. One usually has to wait weeks for that sort of thing.'

He smiled.

'I twisted a few arms and pleaded fast-approaching insanity if I didn't get some speedy improvements in my living conditions.'

They were making small talk, she'd thought, neither of them referring to Saturday night.

'Who have I got first?' she asked the receptionist as she moved towards her consulting room.

'Jess from the post office,' was the reply, and when she buzzed for her to come in Isabel could see that the antibiotics hadn't worked.

'I'm afraid I'm going to have to send you for tests,' she told her. 'I think there could be a formation of a calculus, or a stone, to use a simpler term, in a saliva duct. If I'm right, it will mean a minor operation to remove it.'

The postmistress groaned. 'This is all I need. A face like a balloon and sleepless nights worrying about whether the government will decide to close the post office down.'

'The first problem shouldn't be difficult to solve, if it is what I think it is,' Isabel told her reassuringly, 'and as to the second, it would be terrible if you were closed down. The village store and post office is the centre of our community. We would all be up in arms if it was taken from us. I bought my very first bag of sweets from you and my children will do the same...if I ever find the time to have any.'

Or the man to father them, she thought bleakly, and the memory of Ross's arms around her and his mouth on hers came back like a signpost pointing the way ahead, but it would seem that to him it had said halt.

However, they were Jess's problems they were discussing, not her own, and she asked, 'How long before you get a decision?'

'Soon, I hope,' was the dour reply.

She was a widow with two sons at university. With a mind as sharp as a razor and an endless fount of energy, she ran the store and post office with a brisk sort of efficiency that would be sadly missed if she were to close down. The shop was busy enough, but it was the post office that brought the customers in.

'There's talk of a petition,' Jess said as she got up to go, 'but I hope it won't come to that.'

'So do I,' Isabel told her. 'They would be crazy to close you down and I don't think they will. The ones they have announced for closure so far have been the really small outfits. Your place is big and thriving.'

When she'd gone, Ross came through the communicating door between their two rooms and said, 'That was a long consultation. Problems?'

'No, not really,' Isabel said, taken aback. 'I didn't know you were timing me. I think that Jess has a stone in a saliva duct and I'm passing her on to the hospital. For the rest of the time we were discussing if and when the government might close the post office.'

'And you consider that to be the kind of thing a patient would expect to consult their GP about?'

'Not in the normal scheme of things maybe, but if she isn't sleeping and is very stressed about it then, yes, why not let her express her concerns if it makes her feel better?' she said defiantly.

'Fine,' he said evenly. 'I merely commented on the length of time that Jess had been with you because I thought it might be something serious. But I should have known you would have consulted me if it had been.'

'Yes, I would,' she told him, still on the defensive. 'This place isn't like the impersonal private clinic where you worked before. If Michael Levitt came in about his blood pressure and at the same time wanted to tell me about his financial worries, or how his prize bull wasn't up to scratch, I would listen. Not for too long obviously, but I would lend a listening ear. These people are my friends. They were here when *you* weren't, Ross.'

'All right,' he said. ' You've made your point, but I thought we'd established why *I* wasn't around.'

'Yes, we have, and if someone had told me what it was all about when it was happening, I might have cried a few less tears. The next time I speak to my father I will have a few things to say that he might not like. Sophie said that he'd used me as a pawn and I didn't know what she meant, but I do now. *And* if you are so keen for me to keep to my schedule, I suggest that you let me get on with it.'

'Sure,' he said, 'but before I go, why not let matters rest with your father? In his own autocratic way he did what he thought was best, and who is to say that he wasn't right? Neither of us know why he asked me to come back here, but does it matter? All that we should be concerned about is running the practice to the best of our ability. Agreed?'

It was there again, she thought. The aftermath of Saturday night. The practice, the practice, nothing but the practice!

'Yes, of course,' she agreed smoothly. 'That is what we're here for and you don't need to keep reminding me. I *was* virtually running this place on my own before you appeared on the scene, just in case you've forgotten.'

'I don't forget anything, Izzy,' he told her, and as the colour rose in her cheeks he closed the door that separated them and summoned his next patient.

Ross didn't know why he'd taken Izzy to task about her timing. Every doctor knew that some patients took longer than others and that it balanced itself out with those who were in and out in no time at all.

If he'd wanted to emphasise that practice matters came before personal ones, he'd just made a good start, and ruffled her feathers into the bargain.

She had been right in what she'd said about his previous employment. It *had* been very different, but he'd worked in this place before and shouldn't have forgotten the caring, friendly atmosphere of a country practice.

As the days went by, with midsummer approaching fast, there was sudden activity on wasteland on the outskirts of the village. The fair that came each year in the height of summer had arrived.

Caravans, trailers and huge trucks containing the roundabouts and machinery were trundling into position for a three-day stay, and there was excitement in the air.

'I'd forgotten it was time for the fair,' Ross said as they watched the procession of vehicles go past the surgery window. 'Do you remember how I took you on those bone-shaking bumper cars when I was here, and you felt sick?'

'Yes, I do,' she told him, turning to face him. 'I was mortified, but that was my normal state of mind round about that time.'

'But not now?'

'No. Certainly not now. I don't go in for self-destruction any more.'

She was turning away, ready to make her escape before the conversation took off into something personal, but he took her arm and swivelled her back to face him again. Without loosening his hold, Ross said, 'That being so, let me take you to the fair, Izzy.'

They were almost touching, chest to breast, her startled violet gaze questioning his motives. 'Yes, all right,' she said recklessly, thinking that maybe some time together as just friends would dispel the lingering aftermath of uncertainty that their first, and possibly last, kiss had created.

It was a Thursday and the fair would commence that

night, followed by the same thing on Friday and all day Saturday.

'So when would you like to go?' Ross asked.

'Saturday night,' she said immediately. 'When we won't have been working all day.'

'Fine,' he said. 'I'll call for you at sevenish, if that's all right.'

It would be more than all right, Isabel thought. It would turn a nondescript weekend into something to look forward to. The only blot on the horizon was that the invitation had followed immediately on the heels of her protestation that she was now in charge of her life *and* her emotions.

In truth, the comment was somewhat in the past tense. She *had* been, but that had been before Ross had come back. Since his return her emotions had run riot and her life been turned upside down as with each passing day she was becoming more aware that he was still the only man she wanted to be near.

Later that morning Isabel drove up the hill road to a remote farm lying beneath the shadow of the peaks. She didn't have to make as many house calls now that Ross was in charge, as he did more than his full share of them, but this was one that she wanted to do particularly. Jean Derwent and her family lived at Blackstock Farm, a grim-looking stone building miles away from anywhere. The young mother of two small girls had asked for a visit as she wasn't well enough to go to the surgery.

Her husband, Brian, who was quite a few years older than Jean, had sounded quite grumpy when he'd rung to ask for a doctor to call. Farmers' wives were not supposed to be ill and Jean picked up every virus that was around.

This time it appeared to be serious. She had a hacking cough, her sputum was suspect, her breathing was laboured and she had a temperature.

'How long have you been like this, Jean?' Isabel asked.

'It started a week ago,' she croaked, 'and it's got steadily worse. Brian isn't very pleased as he's such a lot to do around the farm, and having to take the girls to school isn't helping.'

'You should have sent for me before.'

'I know, but I feel such a nuisance.'

'No way are you that,' Isabel told her. 'You've got all the signs of pneumonia.'

'Oh, no,' she wailed.

'Oh, yes, I'm afraid.'

'Brian will hit the roof.'

'That's as maybe, but it's hospital for you, Jean. Where is he at the moment?'

'He'll be seeing to the pigs.'

'I'll go and talk to him.'

Brian looked up when he heard Isabel's footsteps on the flagged yard at the back of the farmhouse.

'Well?' he asked.

'I'm having Jean admitted to hospital,' Isabel told him. 'They'll do tests to confirm it, but it's almost certain that she has pneumonia.'

He was glaring at her.

'Why didn't the new doctor come? I'd like his opinion first. It isn't long since you were just a student.'

'In other words, you are not prepared to take my word for it.'

'Like I say, you've not been doctoring long.'

'Long enough to know pneumonia when I see it,' Isabel told him coolly, 'but if you want a second opinion, I'll ask Dr Templeton to come to see Jean.'

'Aye, do that,' he said.

'Just as long as you realise that you are delaying your wife getting the treatment she needs.'

'What's wrong?' Ross asked when he answered Isabel's call.

'I'm up at the Derwents' place, Blackstock Farm,' she told him. 'Jean Derwent has got a severe bout of pneumonia, but her husband doesn't think I'm qualified enough to know and is asking to see you.'

'Right. I'll come up there straight away. Are you going to wait?'

'No. I'm not. I haven't rung the hospital yet under the circumstances, but I think that is where she needs to be.'

'Dr Templeton is on his way,' she told the disgruntled husband after she'd finished the call. 'So I'll be off once I've said goodbye to your wife. If at any time you need help with the children and feel that you can trust me with them, don't hesitate to ask.'

'Aye, well, we'll see,' he said grudgingly, and Isabel thought that she would rather stay unwed and unloved for ever than be married to a man like Brian Derwent.

Back on the road that stretched across the high flat plateau of the moors, her mind was on the depressing household that she'd just left, and it was only when she was almost opposite him that she saw a man striding through the gorse and windberry bushes in the direction from which she'd just come.

He was tall, bearded and very tanned, dressed in an old khaki greatcoat and with a felt slouch hat on his head. He must have seen her, or at least heard the car, but he gave no indication, just walked on with head bent as if in a world of his own.

It wasn't unusual to see walkers around the village and up on the tops. It was one of the reasons why Sally and Sophie's tea shop was so successful. On the borders of Derbyshire and Cheshire, they were in an area much frequented by those who love the countryside. They came in all shapes and sizes, young and old alike, and normally she wouldn't have looked twice at a lone walker out on the moors, but for some reason she found herself stopping the car and watching until the tall figure in the greatcoat had disappeared from sight.

She was on the point of setting off again when Ross's car appeared on the horizon, so she waited.

'So what's the situation at Blackstock Farm?' he said, winding down the car window as she came to stand beside it.

'A harassed, rather rude farmer with a sick wife. He didn't want to hear what *I* was telling him and asked why *you* hadn't visited her instead of me.'

'And how did you feel about that?'

'I was more aggravated by his manner than his lack of confidence in me, and not sorry to get away. That farm of his gives me the creeps.'

Ross was looking around him. 'I'd forgotten how bleak it can be up here, even in the height of summer.'

'Yes,' she agreed. 'I come here when I want to think. There's a sort of wild magnificence about this place, a timelessness that makes big problems turn into small ones.'

'You're a strange creature, Izzy,' he said gravely. 'I wish life had been kinder to you.'

He watched the fresh colour rise in her cheeks.

'Do you hear me complaining? I might have done once, but not now. I have a job that I love, the cottage which is all mine, Tess and Puss-Puss, who never let me down, my faithful Mini and…' Her voice trailed away.

'You are back in my life,' she'd been about to say, and had then thought better of it. The only reason Ross was taking her to the fair was because he thought she was well and truly over her infatuation with him.

She'd been sure that she was and hadn't wanted him back at the practice, living only minutes away, always at her elbow, back in her life for evermore, but all that was changing, and with it came the fear of making a fool of herself twice over.

Ross didn't comment on the half-finished sentence. He knew what he would have liked her to have said, but that would be presuming too much. The fact that she'd once kissed him with sweet desire didn't mean that Izzy still cared for him. Coming back into her life would have complicated it, rather than enhanced it.

'I'd better get moving,' he said, bringing his mind back to everyday matters, 'or the doubting farmer will have a bone to pick with me too. See you back at the practice, Izzy.' And off he went in the black BMW.

When they met up again after all the house calls had been made, Ross said, 'You were right about Jean Derwent. I've had her admitted to hospital, much to the annoyance of her husband. There was an atmosphere when I was there that I couldn't put my finger on, and I came away with the feeling that there is something odd going on at Blackstock Farm.'

Isabel nodded. 'Yes. I know what you mean. Did you see anything of a tall man wearing an army greatcoat while you were there?'

He looked at her in surprise. 'No. Why do you ask?'

'I saw someone like that walking towards the farm just before we met up on the tops.'

'But surely it isn't unusual to see a lone walker up there.'

'No, of course not. It's just that there was something about him that drew my attention.'

'Maybe it was because it's a bit warm to be wearing that sort of clothing,' he said laughingly. 'We'll have to look out for him coming to the surgery to be treated for heat rash.'

'I told Brian Derwent that I would help with the children if he wanted me to,' she said on a more serious note. 'Did he mention that?'

Ross shook his head.

'No. He said he was going to ask his mother to come up from Carlisle. How long have the Derwents lived at Blackstock Farm? I don't remember them from when I was here before.'

'They bought the place about five years ago and at that time Brian was a different person from what he is now. Enthusiastic, energetic but new to farming. One or two failed crops and Jean's continuing bad health have turned him into the morose person he is now. The children are lovely. Bethany is eight and Charlotte six years, and if his mother is coming to take charge, I will be easier in my mind.'

Ross was frowning.

'You are their GP, Izzy. It is the *health* of your patients that is your concern. Their domestic or business problems are for them to sort out. You can't take the weight of those sort of things onto *your* shoulders. Most of them have family or friends and there is always Social Services. *Our* main concern should be the practice.'

'I'm aware of that,' she said coolly. 'So there is no need to keep reminding me of it. I'm sure that should I not perform my duties satisfactorily, you will be quick to tell me so. Yes, most of those I treat *do* have relations and as to their friends, I am one of them, so perhaps that explains why I am like I am.'

'All right, point taken,' he said. 'It's just that I don't want you to overdo it. You are so alone. That introverted father of yours can't see any further than his next meal, and I know that you are putting up with me on sufferance.'

He was hoping she would deny it, but was about to be disappointed. Isabel wasn't going to admit that she was more aware of him now than she'd ever been.

When Ross called for Isabel on Saturday evening, she invited him into the cottage against her better judgement. She'd had a feeling all along that once he stepped over the threshold it would be another threat to her independence, that his hold on her heartstrings would be tighter, and she wasn't sure if she wanted that.

He had a good look around him and she waited for his comments as he observed the pastel shades on the thick stone walls and the antique-type furniture that she'd bought from various auctions and rummage sales.

'Very nice!' he exclaimed. 'I can see why this place means so much to you. Who lived here before you?'

'One of my father's friends. He was going into sheltered accommodation and sold it to me for a reasonable price. It wasn't as bad as the rooms above the surgery, but I had to do quite a lot of repairs.'

Isabel was smiling as they faced each other across her beamed sitting room. 'You might think I'm too involved with the people round here, but when I come into this place and shut my door, that is it. I don't want to be disturbed. So, you see, you are honoured to have been allowed to see my refuge.'

'Refuge!' he exclaimed. 'That's a bit strong, isn't it? Who is it that you want to get away from?'

'My father, for one. I'd been under his thumb for long enough before I moved in here.'

'And now he's gone without so much as batting an eyelid,' Ross commented wryly. 'The workings of the human mind are complicated, to say the least.'

'He would have been all right if my mother had lived and he hadn't had to bring up a daughter who was as plain as her mother had been beautiful.'

'Stop it!' he said exasperatedly. 'Stop being so maudlin about your looks. Beauty is in the eye of the beholder, Izzy.'

'Is it?' she said slowly, and then added, unable to stop herself, 'And what do *you* see, Ross?'

There was silence for a moment and then he said easily, as if the question were of no consequence, 'I see a woman with hair like ripe corn, eyes like violets and a mouth that's too big beneath a nose that's too small. Does that satisfy you? And if you haven't changed your mind about going to the fair, let's be off.'

'*I* haven't changed my mind about anything,' she said, copying his tone, 'so, yes, let's go. It's our last chance. It will be gone in the morning.'

As they walked towards the sound of jangling music Ross smiled down at his companion. 'It seems like only yesterday that we did this before, but it isn't, is it? It has been seven long years, Izzy. Seven years in which you've changed a lot in some ways, yet not in others. Do you feel that the same applies to me?'

She was panicking, not sure where the conversation was leading. Did Ross guess that his return had awakened all the old longings? That her feelings for him hadn't been put to rest, as she'd thought?

'I don't know whether *you've* changed or not. I can't remember that far back,' she told him untruthfully, and left him to make of that what he would.

CHAPTER SEVEN

TO GET to the field where the fair had been set up they had to pass the new riverside apartments where her father and Millie had taken up residence. Isabel was hoping that Paul wouldn't see Ross and herself together as there was no telling what construction he might put on it. Independent though she now was, he could still get to her in a weak moment.

As it happened, he was watching television and didn't see them strolling past in the summer evening, but Millie did and she was on the phone to him straight away.

'You've just missed them,' she told him breathlessly.

'Who?'

'Your daughter and your ex-partner have just gone past, walking in the direction of the fair, and they seemed to be on the best of terms.'

'Good,' he said. 'I was beginning to think I was wrong in surmising that Isabel still had feelings for Ross Templeton. I wonder whose idea it was to go to the fair together.'

'Does it matter?' Millie said, happy that he was happy for once. 'Sufficient that they are together.'

* * *

'I don't believe it!' Ross exclaimed laughingly, when they arrived at the fair. 'They've got the same bumper cars that they had all that time ago. Are you game, or do you think they might still have the same effect on you?'

'I'll be fine,' she assured him, more concerned about being close to him in the narrow confines of the car than about feeling nauseous.

'You take the wheel,' he said, but after a few bone-shaking collisions with other cars he put his hand over hers and said whimsically, 'Maybe if we steered it together, do you think?'

It was there again, the sense of belonging when he touched her, and Isabel withdrew her hand from beneath his in case he should tune in to her feelings.

Ross was frowning as he manoeuvred the car out of the way of two young girls who seemed to have no sense of direction. Izzy didn't want him to touch her, he thought somberly, though she'd been warm and melting in his arms that night when he'd kissed her on the lane outside her cottage.

But it would seem that things had changed and he knew that he was to blame, because instead of giving in to his feelings he'd spoilt the moment by sounding off about how the practice had to come before anything else.

He'd belittled something new and tender that had sprung up between them as he'd panicked at the thought of making a mess of things a second time.

With his thoughts wandering, he was brought back to the present when they were bumped by a car on either side, sandwiched between two lots of laughing fairground revellers.

When he looked across at Izzy she was laughing, too, her momentary withdrawal put to one side as she teased, 'Do you think I'd better take over again?'

'Not at all,' he said briskly. 'Just watch me.' And with a couple of quick swerves he had the other cars bouncing off them.

With their earlier mood restored, they made the most of what was left of the ride and when it was over Ross said, 'How about the Ferris wheel next?' Then it was darts, catch-pennies, a fistful of candy floss, and Isabel was happier than she'd been in a long time—until she saw Brian Derwent in the distance with Bethany and Charlotte.

Ross had seen him, too, and she answered the question in his eyes by saying, 'I'm just going to have a quick word with Brian. I want to know how Jean is. Or maybe *you* should ask him as he doesn't trust me.'

'He won't thank you,' he said, 'and I'm not getting involved. That sort of discussion should take place at the practice.'

'Even though you thought there was something weird going on at Blackstock Farm?'

'Yes, even though I did think that.'

'If I had a relative who was quite poorly, I would be glad to know that someone cared enough to ask how they were.'

He sighed. 'We were having a great time away from all our cares and duties, and now you want to bring us back to health care. By all means, go and have a word with Derwent, but don't be surprised if he isn't pleased to see you.'

'If you will wait here, I will do that,' she said coolly.

'At least I will have asked.' And off she went to catch up with the trio in front of them.

'How was Jean when you last saw her?' she asked the farmer when she drew level with them.

'The last time I saw her was when they took her to hospital,' he said. 'I'm told that she's improving and will be home some time after the weekend.'

'You haven't been to see her then?'

'Naw. She wouldn't want it if I did.'

'Why ever not?'

'She was on the point of leaving me when she took ill.'

'Leaving you!' Isabel exclaimed. 'Not Jean! She adores you all.'

'Oh, aye? The girls maybe, but not me. She's going to go off with the botanist fellow who's rented a cottage just down the track from us as soon as she's better.'

'Are you sure?' she croaked.

'Yes, I'm sure,' he told her dryly. 'She spends more time with him, studying plants and things, than she does with me, and now, if you've quite finished poking your nose into our affairs, we'll be off.' And before she'd had time to gather her wits he had gone.

'Well?' Ross said when she went back to join him. 'What was all that about? It took him long enough to tell you how his wife was.'

'Brian was explaining that Jean intends leaving him and going off with some botanist who's rented a cottage somewhere up on the tops near their farm,' she told him, amazement still upon her.

'Ah! So that's why he's so uptight and miserable. Or is that how he is normally? If that's the case, he's probably asked for it.'

'Brian can be a bit sombre,' she told him, 'but he's had a few serious setbacks since they bought the farm and he's a proud man. The type who won't want to admit defeat.'

'Or accept that his wife is leaving him,' Ross suggested.

'Yes, definitely that,' she agreed. 'But what Brian has just told me doesn't apply to the Jean I know. She is a loving mother *and* I would have said a loyal wife. One thing is for sure, she won't leave the children behind and, knowing Brian, he won't let her take them with her.'

Risking another rebuff, Ross took her hand in his and tucked it into the crook of his arm. Distracted by what she'd just been told, Isabel let it stay there. She'd spoilt what had been a wonderful evening by accosting Brian Derwent, she thought, and looking up into a sky that was now like dark velvet she said, 'You were right. I should have minded my own business and not brought the practice into our free time. Much as you want it to come before everything else, you didn't want me to do it. But believing that I knew best, I took no notice, and now I won't be able to stop thinking about the Derwents.'

'You did what you did because you are what you are,' he said quietly. 'But as I've already said, it's the health of your patients that should be your concern. Their other problems are *theirs* alone. Did anyone give themselves sleepless nights worrying over you when you needed someone? Certainly not your father, I would imagine.'

He wasn't going to tell her that he knew one person, living in a far-away land, who had lain sleepless many a night on her account. Wishing he'd handled everything differently and been grateful for any news of the girl who had sobbed her heart out in his arms on the morning he'd left the village.

'I was told that I mustn't discuss it with anyone,' she said dryly. 'The people who knew me could only guess what ailed me. But it's all in the past.' She withdrew her hand from the crook of his arm. 'And that is where I want it to stay.'

It was true. She wanted a new beginning for them without any cobwebs hanging over it, without any pain involved, and so far Ross had shown no sign of feeling the same. He was brisk and efficient with regard to the practice and kind and tolerant with herself most of the time, but she could tell that he was wary.

They were subdued on the walk home and when they reached the cottage she turned to him and said dejectedly, 'I don't know why you bother with me, Ross.'

He was smiling now.

'Hey! Where has the liberated young doctor disappeared to? Don't feel down just because you were kind enough to enquire about a sick patient. I imagine that as it's Sunday tomorrow you'll be off to the hospital to see Jean Derwent, whether her husband likes it or not.'

Her answering smile was rueful. 'You read my mind. I wouldn't have gone normally. I'm not *that* eager to butt into my patients' private lives, but after what Brian told me I have to speak to Jean. If what he said is true, there has to be a very good reason for it, and as she has no relatives of her own she might be glad of someone to talk to.'

'You don't have to explain your motives to me,' he said levelly. 'As long as you put in an appearance at the practice on weekdays, what you do with your weekends is your own affair.'

'It's happening again!' she said exasperatedly.

'What is?'

'Another unnecessary reminder of where my priorities should lie. *I* won't let *you* down ever, Ross.' And on that firm promise she went in and closed the door behind her.

The moment she'd slid the catch across, Isabel wished she hadn't been in such a hurry to leave him and she opened the door again, but Ross was already striding briskly down the lane without a backward glance, and she thought uncomfortably that she'd been rude and belligerent when all she wanted was to be at peace with him.

She told herself that she would apologise when next she saw him. Tell him that she hadn't meant to sound so aggressive. But that wouldn't be until Monday and as she went up the steep stairs that led to her bedroom she was wondering if they would ever share the same bed in this world.

Don't, she cautioned herself. Don't start going along that road. If Ross hadn't wanted to go home he would have let you know. He was probably relieved to get back to the peace of his own place after spending the last few hours putting up with your fads and fancies. Concentrate on what you're going to say to Jean Derwent tomorrow, instead of wishing for the moon.

As Isabel approached the small side ward where the farmer's wife had been placed, her step faltered. Through the open door she could see that Jean had a visitor. The man that she'd seen striding across the moor was seated at the side of the bed, the khaki greatcoat that he'd worn when Izzy had seen him previously draped over a chair.

'Dr West!' Jean exclaimed with no signs of embarrassment when she saw her. 'How nice of you to come.'

Her visitor was getting to his feet and Isabel said quickly, 'Please, don't go on my account.'

He smiled. 'I was going in any case. I'll leave you ladies to it. Bye for now, Jean.' And lifting his greatcoat off the chair, he went.

'Who is that?' Izzy asked when he'd gone. 'Is he the man that you're going to leave Brian for?'

The woman in the bed groaned.

'Is that what he's been telling you? His name is Simon Stoddard. He's a botanist renting a house near the farm. We've discovered that we have a common interest—plant life. That crazy husband of mine isn't thinking straight these days. Of course I'm not going to leave him and the girls.

'Brian was jealous about the time I was spending with Simon. We had a big row and in the heat of it I told him I would rather be with Simon than have to put up with a joyless husband. Now he's got the idea that I'm going to leave him, and I'm so fed up with his bad temper that I'm letting him stew for a while. It will teach him a lesson.'

'Thank goodness,' Isabel breathed. 'I was worried when he told me that you were splitting up. I'd always thought that you and Brian were solid in spite of his gripes.'

Jean smiled. 'We are. They're sending me home tomorrow as my lungs are clear now. I'll put him out of his misery then.'

'And the botanist? Are you still going to keep seeing him?'

'No, sadly, as he's a very interesting fellow. But Brian has had enough to cope with since we bought the farm and I know just how much he loves me in spite of his bad temper.'

When Isabel left the hospital she was smiling. She couldn't wait to tell Ross that all would soon be resolved at Blackstock Farm. As she pulled out onto the road she saw Simon waiting at the bus stop and pulled up alongside the man who had been the unwitting cause of the farmer's anger.

'I'll be driving past your place,' she told him. 'Do you want a lift?'

'Er…yes. I would be very much obliged,' he said in mild surprise.

Isabel smiled. She could have kissed him for not wanting to take Jean away from her family.

'I'm one of the GPs at the village practice,' she explained.

'Ah, I see,' he replied. 'I've been waiting here for some time and no public transport has shown up, so your offer is most welcome.'

She gave him a quick sideways glance as he got into the car. Brian Derwent was far more attractive than the bearded botanist, but she would like to bet that he wouldn't come out on top when it came to patience and fortitude. Thank goodness that tomorrow Jean was going to put an end to her husband's misery and tell him that *he* was the only man she wanted.

After dropping Simon off, Isabel pulled out onto the road that led across the moors before dipping down into the village. After she'd gone a couple of miles she suddenly sat more upright in her seat. She could see flames leaping into the air in the distance and knew they could only be coming from one place—Blackstock Farm.

Within minutes the farm buildings came into sight and when she pulled up in the farmyard she froze with horror. The big barn at the side of the farmhouse was alight and up in the hayloft, silhouetted against the flames, was Brian.

'Oh, my God,' she breathed. 'Has he gone over the edge and set the place alight?' She flung herself out of the car and looked around her for any signs of the children. Please, don't let them be in there with him, she prayed as she ran towards the barn door.

As she prepared to wrench it open an arm came from behind and dragged her away and Ross's voice cried, 'Stay back, Izzy. I'll go and get him.'

'What are *you* doing here?' she cried. 'And where are the children?'

'What I'm doing here doesn't matter, and the children have gone somewhere with Brian's mother. Now, stand back, Izzy, I'm going to force the door open.'

'I'm coming with you.'

'You are not! Don't even think of it. Ring the fire services if you want to make yourself useful, but before that slam the door shut the moment I've gone inside.' With that last instruction he put his shoulder against it and as it swung back he plunged inside.

Isabel was desperate to follow him, but what Ross had said made sense, and with fingers that shook she shut the door and then phoned the emergency services on her mobile.

She could see him up there beside the farmer now, grasping his arm and pulling him towards the ladder, but Brian wouldn't budge, and her fear increased. As she watched, transfixed with the horror of the scene before her, she saw him sag to his knees as the smoke began to affect him. Seizing the opportunity, Ross heaved him upright again, slung him over his shoulder and disappeared into the flames with his limp burden.

Please, don't let Ross die in there, she prayed.

Her first frenzied prayer had been for the children who thankfully weren't around, and now she was praying for the man she loved. She'd lost him once before, but had at least known he had been alive somewhere in the world. If the fire took him, Ross would be lost to her for ever, and the despair she'd felt before would be nothing in comparison.

After what seemed like an eternity, though it could only have been minutes, he came staggering out of the blazing barn, and as he laid the farmer on the stone slabs of the farmyard she was beside him in a flash.

Ross was propping himself up against the drystone wall nearby, gasping for breath, with his hair and eyebrows singed and his face bright red from the heat of the flames. But from Brian Derwent there was no movement.

As she bent over him Isabel gave a sigh of relief. There was a pulse. He was breathing wheezily, but breathing nevertheless. He had been in the barn for some minutes before Ross had gone in to get him, and obviously the smoke had affected him quite seriously.

He had burns down one side of his face and she wished she had her case with her. As if reading her thoughts, Ross croaked, 'Mine is in the car.'

'Where are you parked?'

'Round the back.'

As she got to her feet two things happened. Brian Derwent made a weak moaning sound and the sirens of the emergency services could be heard, drawing nearer with every second.

Ross was still leaning against the wall, coughing and gasping, and as soon as the paramedics had taken charge of Brian she went to him. Gazing into a pair of red-rimmed eyes, she told him, 'You need to be treated for smoke inhalation. The ambulance crew are putting Brian into the ambulance at this moment and we're going with them.'

She glanced across to where the men of the fire service already had their hoses playing onto the burning building. 'There's nothing else we can do here. They'll have to break the news to Brian's mother and the girls, should they return while we're gone, and once we get to the hospital I will have the unenviable task of telling Jean that he probably tried to burn the place down. She isn't going to feel exactly guilt-free when she hears that, I'm afraid, as she had no intention of leaving Brian. She was just letting him think that to teach him a lesson.'

'What a mess,' he croaked. 'He was all set for staying up there. I don't know what I would have done if the smoke hadn't got to him.'

'Yes, I know,' she said gently as she helped him across to the ambulance. 'I have never been so terrified in my life as I waited to see if you would come out of there alive.'

He managed a smile. 'Not as terrified as I would

have been if I hadn't got there in time to stop *you* from going in.' He became serious again. 'You were right with your ideas of out-of-hours surgery care. I should have realised earlier that Derwent was on the edge, that he needed counselling. That was why I happened to be here when you arrived. I'd come to have a chat with him and was going to suggest he make an appointment to see me at the surgery for some antidepressants. When I asked him where the children were he said they'd gone out with his mother and wouldn't be back for a while.'

'He asked if I'd like a coffee, which I thought was a sign that he wasn't feeling quite so aggressive, and went off into the kitchen. But while I sat there like a fool, waiting for him to make it, he must have slipped out of the back door and run across to the barn. It would have taken just a few slurps out of a petrol can and a lighted match for the fire to get going.'

'It could have been worse, I suppose,' Isabel said glumly. 'It could have been the farmhouse that went up in flames. At least they'll have somewhere to live.'

The paramedics were ready for them and once they were all settled inside the ambulance it was off, with Brian lying on one of the stretchers, being given oxygen. His breathing was too laboured for him to be able to speak and if he had been able to she wouldn't have wanted to hear what he had to say. If this man was supposed to love his family he had a funny way of showing it, she thought grimly.

The only good thing about the afternoon's horrendous happenings was that he hadn't taken the children into the barn with him.

Anger was rising in her. Ross had risked his life to

get him out of there. She hoped Brian would realise that once he was in a calmer state of mind.

As the ambulance pulled up outside Accident and Emergency, Jean, her mother-in-law, and the children were coming out of the main entrance and making their way towards the car park.

They stopped in surprise when Isabel called across to them, and her mouth went dry at the thought of what she had to tell Jean as she went over to them.

'They've got Brian in the ambulance,' she said.

'Why? What's wrong? Has he had an accident?' Jean asked anxiously.

'He was all right when we left the farm earlier,' his mother said in alarm.

Isabel took a deep breath. Ross had said that he thought she was right to be there for her patients whenever the occasion arose, be it in the practice or outside of it, but she could do without moments like this.

'We think he tried to kill himself,' she told the two women. 'It looks as if he set fire to the barn while he was inside. Dr Templeton was there and he got him out in the nick of time. You were just a few hours too late with what you had to tell him, Jean.'

'The crazy fool!' his mother said frantically, but Jean wasn't there to hear. She was halfway across the hospital forecourt to where her husband was being lifted out of the ambulance, her face white with horror.

The two doctors were back at the practice. Ross had been checked over for smoke inhalation and been allowed home, and Isabel had insisted on going back to his place to keep an eye on him for what was left of Sunday.

Brian had been kept in for observation. He would be seeing a psychologist the following day, and would be receiving a visit from the police to ascertain what had happened.

They'd got a taxi home as both of their cars were still at the farm and during the journey the day's events, all of them crystal clear, had gone through Isabel's mind, starting with her visit to Jean in the early afternoon, then taking the botanist home, followed by the awful sight of flames in a summer sky.

Then it had all speeded up into a nightmare. The blazing barn, the man standing up in the hayloft and Ross appearing out of nowhere and dragging her back when she would have gone in.

It had been horrendous enough up to then, but when Ross had gone inside the burning building sheer terror had taken over at the thought that she might lose him.

That she hadn't was something she would be grateful for to her dying day and if he never wanted *her* as she wanted *him* she would accept it in that same spirit of gratitude.

'I'm going to make a meal,' she said as soon as they got in, resisting the urge to hold him close and never let him go. 'I'm starving.'

Ross was on the point of heading for the shower to get the grime from the smoke off him and he nodded. 'Good idea. I'm feeling peckish myself. Fire rescue must give one an appetite.'

'Don't,' she said with a shudder. 'That foolish man has really messed things up for all of them. It's surprising how some people can take any amount of stress and others just can't cope with it at all.'

'It was bizarre, Jean being on the point of leaving the hospital when we got there, wasn't it?' he commented. 'We almost missed her.'

'She wasn't supposed to be going home until tomorrow,' Isabel told him, 'but because of what I'd said about Brian, she'd persuaded them to discharge her a day early. Yet sadly she didn't get there in time to put his fears to rest, and look what she has facing her now. Knowing what he's like, I'm surprised she let him think she was going to leave him. But the damage is done.'

'At least he made sure that no one but himself was going to be at risk.'

'Except you!'

'Yes. But he didn't ask me to go in after him, did he? Though now he knows that his wife had no intention of leaving him, he might be glad that I did. What would you have done if I'd perished in there?' he asked suddenly. 'Not spent the rest of your life grieving, I hope.'

He knows, she thought! Ross knows that I love him and is telling me in a roundabout sort of way that I need to get over it.

She laughed and it sounded shrill to her ears.

'I wouldn't have gone into a convent, if that's what you mean, but I would have remembered you always as someone very brave,' she said lightly, and hoped that it sounded convincing.

If she hadn't been so flustered at the way the conversation was going she might have thought he looked disappointed, but to hide her confusion she'd turned her attention to the meal she'd promised him and was investigating the contents of the fridge.

By the time that Ross had reappeared looking scrubbed

and clean, she was ready to take steaks from under the grill and serve the vegetables to go with them. When they sat down to eat, they were back on safe subjects, such as when the decorator was due to finish and what kind of furniture Ross was going to replace her father's old stuff with.

As the sun sank below the horizon and night drew in, Isabel felt mental and physical exhaustion begin to take its toll. It had been a day that she would never forget, and once she'd tidied the kitchen after the meal and made sure that Ross wasn't having any worrying after-effects from the fire, she told him that she was going home.

'I'm very tired,' she told him, 'and Tess and Puss-Puss will be waiting to be fed. They will be thinking I've deserted them.'

'I wouldn't imagine that *you've* ever deserted anyone or anything,' he said quietly. 'Which is more than some of the rest of us can say. Sleep well in your pretty cottage, Izzy.'

He knew that she had no idea how much he would like her to stay, snuggled up against him through the night. But just because once again they'd been brought together in circumstances connected with other people, it didn't mean that he wasn't going to carry on with the waiting game that he'd played for so long.

'How can you expect me to sleep with the problems of the Derwent family going round in my mind?' she protested tiredly.

'When I said that I'd changed my ideas and understood you looking after the concerns of our patients outside surgery hours, it didn't include you lying sleepless all night on their account. That will achieve nothing for either you or them.'

'Easier said than done,' she said, her hand on the door latch.

'I'm coming with you,' he said, 'and once I've seen you safely inside I won't be long out of bed myself. And, Izzy...'

'What?'

'I don't want to be reminded that you are quite capable of seeing yourself home. That you've done it a thousand times and nobody cared a damn.'

'It's true.'

He put a finger over her lips.

'Shush! From now on, when you are with me and it is dark, I take you home. Understood?'

As he looked into her face he saw tears in the beautiful eyes looking up into his and he asked gently, 'What's wrong? The last thing I want is to upset you.'

'You're making me feel as if I matter,' she said, forcing back the tears, 'and it feels strange and unsettling.'

It's something you are going to have to get used to, he thought, and one day I will tell you why.

CHAPTER EIGHT

WHEN Isabel called in at the post office on her way to the surgery the next morning, Jess said, 'It's all around the village that Brian Derwent set his barn on fire yesterday. That he was trying to commit suicide and that Ross Templeton saved him.'

'Yes, Ross went into the barn and brought him out safely,' she said uncomfortably, making no comment about the rest of what Jess had said as she had no wish to fill in the details of the tragic circumstances for the benefit of the locals. 'Who told you?'

'Ross went round to his mother's late last night to let her and Sophie know what had happened. He didn't want them hearing it from another source and being anxious on his behalf. It seems like a sad state of affairs at the Derwents',' the postmistress went on. 'If he was having money worries, there would always have been someone in the community who would help tide him over.'

'It was more because Jean was ill that Brian got himself in a state,' Isabel explained. 'I think the fire was due more to carelessness than anything else. That he lit a cigarette and didn't put it out properly, and because he had so much on his mind when the hay began to blaze he just stood there, rooted to the spot.'

'Oh! So that's what happened,' Jess said, her interest waning as Isabel's not-strictly-true version of events gave the story a new slant. 'Well, whatever it was, that fellow has always been a loser.'

'Not in everything,' Isabel reminded her. 'He has a loving wife and two beautiful children. Jean will get him through this. She may not be the stronger of the two physically, but she has more stamina mentally.' And on that more positive note she made a speedy departure before she was forced to be sparing with the truth again.

Ross was already there when she got to the surgery, sporting his singed hair and eyebrows and a slightly redder than usual complexion, but apart from that he seemed all right.

'So *did* you sleep?' he asked when she appeared at the door of his consulting room.

'Yes, surprisingly,' she told him. 'Did you?'

'Mmm, after a fashion, with a few nightmares thrown in. The police have just been on the phone to say they'll be coming to ask some questions later.'

'I told Jess at the post office that it was an accident from a lighted cigarette, which I suppose was a stupid thing to do.'

He shook his head. 'I shall have to tell them the truth, but will emphasise that I'd gone to see him because of his mental state. That he was suffering from acute depression and would not have been responsible for his actions. It might mean him going into psychiatric care for a while, but otherwise that should be all.'

'But who will look after the farm while that is happening?' she said anxiously.

'I don't know, but it will be an ideal opportunity for the local community to rally round if they are as supportive as you say they are. And by the way, what was the result regarding Jess's suspected saliva duct blockage? I'm taking it that it's been sorted. I was in the post office the other day and the swelling was no longer visible.'

'It turned out to be what I suspected,' she told him. 'She was in hospital for the day while they did a minor op to remove the blockage. Hopefully that will be the last of it. If it isn't, I'll have to refer her back to them.'

'I wish that one of my patients this morning had something so easily fixed,' he said sombrely, with his glance on the surgery clock. It was coming up to half past eight.

'Why? Who is it?'

'The young lad whose parents own the Pheasant. Do you know the family?'

'No. I'm afraid I don't. They only took over recently. What is wrong with the child?'

'Young Jake is as bright as a button, an adorable kid, but he was born with a severe facial deformity. His jaw bone was damaged at birth and it's a source of great anxiety to his parents. So far no one has come up with any solutions and the poor kid has to eat through a straw, has difficulty talking and cleaning his teeth and has a permanently fixed expression.

'Naturally his parents are keen to do something about it, but no one has been able to suggest what. While I was staying at the hotel when I first came back here, I became aware of Jake's problem and his parents and I got talking. I told them about an amazing new implant at present undergoing trials, which is already helping children like him.

'It seems that a child in Russia has had the whole of a deformed jaw bone removed and the implant put in its place, and almost immediately she could eat, laugh and talk, where none of that was possible before.

'The introduction of it has been a joint effort by British and Russian scientists. It's made of a honeycomb-like polymer that bonds to the bone and the big advantages are that it's light, flexible, tough and, believe it or not, cheap.

'Needless to say, Jake's parents were very interested in what I had to tell them and are coming in this morning to bring me up to date with what progress they've made regarding their son being given the implant.'

'Poor child.' she said softly. 'It's bad enough being plain, but to have that sort of disfigurement is awful.'

Ross was out of his seat behind the desk in a flash, and before she could move he was gripping her by the forearms, his eyes, still red-rimmed from the fire, bright with irritation.

'I could shake you, Izzy West!' he hissed. 'I am sick of hearing you complaining about your looks. What is it that you want? To be told all the time that you're a raving beauty? Isn't it more important that you're clever and kind, and beneath the face that you are always complaining about are curves so much in the right places that the average male couldn't help but want to see more of them?'

She looked at him wide-eyed, amazed that a casual comment should have brought about such an irate reaction. He was still gripping her arms and she didn't shake him off. She could feel the heat of his hands through the sleeves of the lightweight top she was wearing and, unable to resist the opportunity, she said coolly, 'But *you*, it would seem, are not the average male.'

'Oh, I'm that all right,' he said through gritted teeth, 'but I'm also someone who has learnt by his past mistakes.'

'And you think I haven't.'

It was there again, she thought. The warning that even if *she* was ready to try again, *he* wasn't.

There was a footstep outside in the passage. Freeing her from his grasp, he turned away and said, 'Let's get the day under way, shall we?'

'By all means,' she replied in the same cool tone. 'Never let it be said that we talked about ourselves for a moment.' And off she went.

As he called in his first patient Ross was thinking that he'd just behaved badly with someone that he had no wish to hurt ever again. Why hadn't he told Izzy that to him she was perfect in every way, instead of ranting at her like a madman?

In spite of the coolness that she wore like a protective cloak, he knew that she was still vulnerable because of past hurts bestowed upon her by her father and himself, and much as he would have liked to have kissed her until she understood that she *was* beautiful, he'd kept a tight hold on his feelings and stayed calm, even though the soft warmth of her beneath his hands had made it difficult.

When he'd first come back and met the confident young doctor who amazingly wasn't spoken for in any shape or form, he'd been on a high. He'd told himself that maybe their time had come but, remembering what had happened before, he'd been prepared to wait for as long as it took for Izzy to trust him again.

But he hadn't been prepared for her father taking a back seat in her life so soon after his arrival, which had simplified everything, and neither had he expected her to affect him so much that waiting was the last thing he wanted to do.

He wanted to court her, cherish her, so that she might be as confident in her private life as she was in the career that she'd chosen. Maybe it was time he did that. He'd make a start by inviting Izzy out for the evening and take it from there.

'Mornin', Doctor,' old Sam Shuttleworth said as he lowered himself slowly into a chair. He'd been a lockkeeper in his youth on the canal that was the other well-loved waterway in the village, and now lived with his daughter behind her florist's shop.

As Ross returned his greeting he was observing the old man's restricted mobility of movement and knew that a moment's impatience had turned what had been a sprightly octogenarian into someone who needed a stick to make his laboured progress around the village.

Instead of waiting until the traffic lights in the middle of the main street had been green, Sam had scuttled across while they were red when there had been a lull in the traffic and had been knocked down by a car that he hadn't seen coming.

Under the circumstances he'd got off lightly, with just a broken tibia, but at his age it was not something he was going to gallop away with. Even though the fracture had slowly healed, he was now crippled with arthritis and had lost the misguided confidence that had taken him into the road when he should have stayed on the pavement.

'So how are the aches and pains today?' Ross asked the old man.

'Same as usual,' Sam grunted. 'I need some more tablets but your receptionist woman behind the counter said that I had to see either you or Dr West first.'

'Yes, that is so,' he confirmed. 'As you know, we don't hand out tablets like sweets. We need to know periodically if the patient's condition has changed and if the medication should be increased or reduced, or maybe changed to something else. So first of all we'll see how your blood pressure looks, what your heart has to say when I sound it and if your chest is clear. The last time you came in and saw Dr West, you had an infection.'

'Aye. I did, and I got a telling-off for not looking where I was going. Young Isabel said that she'd noticed that we old 'uns, men in particular, with plenty of time on their hands, are always in a rush and she wanted to know why.'

'And what was *your* excuse?' Ross asked, hiding a smile at the thought of Izzy sorting out this crotchety old soul.

'With me it was usually that I was in a hurry to get to the pub for opening time, or back to the television, or something like that. That day, Emma, my daughter, had asked me to go to the grocer's for her before I'd read the morning paper. I don't like to be disturbed until I've read it from back to front, so I was in a rush to get back.'

'With unfortunate consequences.'

'Aye. I don't need reminding. So *are* you going to examine me or not?' he asked grumpily, and Ross thought that if the mobility had gone, the impatience hadn't.

When the family from the Pheasant followed him into the consulting room he thought what a difference there was between the two patients—one an irascible old man who was totally to blame for what now ailed him, and the other an innocent child, the victim of damage at birth.

'So, what progress have you made?' he asked as Jake's mother and father seated themselves opposite and the child squatted down on the floor to play with a toy he'd brought with him.

'Some,' his father replied, 'but things are not moving as fast as we would like.'

Ross nodded.

'That I can believe, and the reason will be because the implant is still in its trial stages. But take heart from the fact that Jake is being considered for it, even if you have to take him to Russia and pay for it.'

'We would take him to the ends of the earth if we could make his life easier,' his mother said. 'And if we have to pay, we'll find the money from somewhere. The consultant that you sent us to is doing all he can to help. He's examined Jake and pronounced him an ideal recipient for the implant, but there seems to be such a lot of red tape to get through first.'

'Whatever the result,' his father said, 'we won't forget how you brought hope into our lives from just a chance conversation, and the moment we have anything further to tell you we'll be down here. We've been down this road a few times before and been told that nothing could be done, but now, for the first time, we have hope but we're not going to sit back and wait for ever.'

With her glance on her son, who was absorbed in the toy that he'd brought with him, his mother said, 'Jake is our only child and we love him dearly. I had a very difficult birth, which was to blame for his deformed jaw, and I've felt guilty ever since.'

'Don't feel guilty, it's no one's fault,' Ross said gently. 'The consultant I referred you to is top in his field, and he'll do all he can to get the health authorities to consider Jake's case.'

'We're due to see him again soon and maybe he'll have some news for us then,' Jake's father informed Ross.

'I'll keep my fingers crossed for you,' Ross told him, 'and remember, if you do get the go-ahead, ask the hospital to explain every detail of what is going to happen as something as new as this isn't routine surgery. And don't forget I'm always here if you want to talk.'

When they'd gone he sat deep in thought before summoning his next patient. Perhaps he should tell Izzy the same thing, that he would always be there if ever she wanted to talk. But after losing his cool earlier when she'd commented on her looks, he had a feeling that a heart to heart was not going to be on her agenda at the present time.

But at least he could discuss practice matters with her and tell her what Jake's parents had said. As GPs they were always interested in anything new that would help their patients and he knew that she'd been touched by the little boy's predicament, even though her comments had made him fly off the handle.

As he'd watched Jake playing contentedly with his toy, quite unaware that he was the subject of the discussion, Ross had tried to imagine how he would feel if Jake had been his son, his and Izzy's. Rather that the parent should suffer than the child any time, he thought, and yet it was the young ones who seemed to cope the best with life's afflictions.

The police had arrived. Izzy had seen the squad car outside on the surgery forecourt and wondered what Ross was saying to them. She knew that while still telling the truth he would do his best to play down Brian Derwent's behaviour of the day before for the sake of the man himself and his wife and children, but in the telling he would also have to consider just how much of a threat the depressed farmer was to those around him.

She was hoping that they wouldn't want to talk to her without her knowing what Ross had said to them, but as he'd pointed out when they'd discussed it earlier, it would have to be the truth and following on that would be the hospital's decision regarding the state of Brian Derwent's mind.

It went without saying that she was going to talk to Jean at the first opportunity, to see if there was anything she could do to help, but it would have to wait until later in the day when she was out on her rounds. In the meantime she was doing her best not to think about how Ross had acted when she'd been commenting on her lack of good looks.

It had been merely a statement of fact, she thought wryly. She hoped she hadn't made him think she was fishing for compliments, and as he couldn't tell a lie about her looks he'd decided to compliment her on her figure.

When he opened the communicating door between their two rooms and beckoned her in, Isabel knew that it had been a vain hope that the police wouldn't want to talk to her.

A young policewoman and an older constable were seated opposite Ross and when she went in they rose to their feet.

'Just a few questions about the fire at Blackstock Farm, if you don't mind, Dr West,' the constable said ponderously. 'We've heard Dr Templeton's version and now we'd like to hear yours.'

'There's not a lot to tell,' she said smoothly, deciding that she was not going to be intimidated in any way. 'As Dr Templeton will have told you, we have been concerned about Brian Derwent over the last week or so. He had been having problems with the farm and then his wife mistakenly gave him the impression that she intended leaving him, and that was the last straw.

'He is inclined to get easily depressed. If he was responsible for the fire, we both think that it came from a mindless moment of despair and feel sure that now he knows that his wife hasn't stopped loving him and had no intention of leaving him, he will be all right. After all, it was his own property that he damaged and no one was hurt.'

'Quite so,' the constable said dryly, 'but if your colleague here hadn't risked his life, the consequences could have been disastrous. We shall be sending in a report to the chief constable.'

Isabel hadn't looked at Ross while she'd been speaking. She didn't want the police to think they were concocting a story that they'd agreed on previously, neither did she want to see anything in his expression that would make her falter in what she had to say.

'It was a brave thing that you did,' the policewoman told Ross with what Isabel thought was overdone admiration.

He smiled across at her. 'I was only thankful that I was there. I'd gone to see Brian to ask him to come to the surgery so that I could prescribe some sort of antidepressants.'

'And what were *you* doing at Blackstock Farm?' the constable asked Isabel in the same dry tone.

'I was driving across the moors, saw the flames in the sky and went to investigate.'

He unbuttoned his top pocket and put away his notebook. "It would seem that it was Brian Derwent's lucky day. All the GPs of the neighbourhood converging on his property. I live in the centre of the town and getting a doctor out to see you is like getting blood out of a stone. And as for them arriving unasked-for!' He turned to his companion. 'Come on, Jackie. We've got all the info we need.' Taking her glance off Ross, the young policewoman followed him out into Reception.

When they'd gone the two doctors observed each other uneasily and Isabel said, 'I hope I didn't contradict anything you'd said.'

'No, you were unflinchingly convincing,' he said, with the beginning of a smile. 'And let's face it, we told no lies. It was just a case of putting our own points of view for the Derwents' sake, and don't forget that even though the police are unlikely to prosecute, the farmer won't be out of trouble. He might get a bill from the fire services, and then there's the possibility of psychiatric care.'

'I'm going to call at the farm while I'm out on my

rounds,' she told him. 'I'm anxious to know what's going on there and how Jean is coping.'

He didn't reply, just nodded, and then into the silence said, 'Are you doing anything special tonight?'

For a moment there was surprise in the violet eyes looking into his and then it was gone as, ignoring a faster beating heart, she asked coolly, 'Why?'

'I'd like to take you out for a meal.'

'Why?'

'Does there have to be a reason?'

'Yes, when it concerns us.'

'All right, then. It will be to say thank you for supporting me during these last weeks while I've been settling in,' he said casually. 'It can't have been easy.'

'It hasn't,' she told him with candour, but didn't elaborate further.

There was no way she was going to tell Ross just how much her world had been turned upside down again when he'd reappeared out of the blue. It might end up in her admitting that she'd never stopped loving him. That she'd discovered that what she'd written off as a schoolgirl crush had been the real thing, strong, true and passionate. If that didn't put him on the defensive, nothing would.

He was raising a questioning eyebrow. 'So have we got a date?'

'Yes,' she said in the same cool tone. 'I'd like to dine out. Where are you going to take me?'

He would have loved to have shattered her calm by saying 'To bed?', but he'd shirked the issue and told Izzy that the invitation was just a way of saying thanks. So he would have to see what some time together in an atmospheric setting brought, if anything.

'Sophie tells me there's a new restaurant up on the hill road that is highly recommended. Shall we try there?'

She shrugged.

'Yes, whatever. I don't mind where we go, but don't make it too early in the evening as I'll need to shower and change, feed my animals and wash my breakfast pots when I get in.'

He sighed.

'I can see that you are just bursting to go out with me. Are you sure you don't have to clean the windows or run over the lawn with the mower before we go?'

In his mind's eye he could see Sophie's expression when he'd asked if she could suggest somewhere special for whenever he was ready to move things along between Izzy and himself.

'Why? Who would you be thinking of taking out?' she'd asked in her abrupt way. 'I would hope that it's Isabel West, but only if you aren't going to be messing her around this time. Your mother and me would love to see some young ones around the place before we both pass on.'

'Hey, steady on, Sophie,' he'd exclaimed laughingly. 'All I did was ask you where the best eating places were, apart from your delightful tearooms.'

'Get away with you,' she'd said with a chuckle. 'Flattery will get you everywhere. But think about what I've said. Isabel won't be around for ever. One day some fellow will appear and sweep her off her feet.'

'And why do you think I would have my sights on Izzy?'

'Maybe it's because I've got eyes in my head,' she'd

told him, and had gone on to say, 'There's a place up near the tops that's very popular. An old barn that somebody has converted into a tasteful restaurant that blends in with the area.'

'And where exactly is it?' he'd asked.

'It's near the Kissing Stone.'

'And where and what is that? I don't remember it from before.'

'You might have done if you'd been into kissing,' she'd replied. 'It's a big, black rock, smooth as silk, in the middle of the moors. Nobody knows how it came to be there. It's nothing like the local limestone. The legend has it that lovers who kiss while touching it will be together for ever.'

And now he was taking her advice. Making the first move towards his second takeover in a matter of weeks. The first had been important, had meant a lot to him, but he knew that it was Izzy that he'd really come back for.

During the first years of his self-imposed exile he'd been racked with many emotions, none of them pleasant. Amongst them had been guilt because he hadn't seen the signs that a young and vulnerable woman had been falling in love with him, and there'd been sadness inside him, too, for the hurt he'd caused her.

He had always been able to attract women but had never found the one that made his heart beat faster—and that had included Paul West's lonely daughter. And though memories of the trauma from all that time ago had never left him, he hadn't made any definite plans to come back until he'd got the elderly GP's letter regarding the practice. It had only been then that he'd known how much he'd wanted to see Izzy again. That he hadn't laid to rest the ghost of the sobbing girl who had begged him to stay.

When he'd met a composed young doctor who on the surface was nothing like the Izzy West he'd known before, he had realised that the reason why he'd never had any serious relationships over the past seven years had been standing before him, unattached, unperturbed and unaware of what she was doing to his heartstrings.

'I thought I'd reserve a table at the place that Aunt Sophie recommended,' he told her, dragging his thoughts back to the present. 'It is a barn that's been turned into a restaurant.'

'Sounds nice,' she told him. 'Shall we say eight o'clock?'

'Will you have finished all your chores by then?'

'Yes.'

'Right. Eight o'clock it is and, Izzy...I'm really looking forward to us having some time together.'

Feeling that she'd been playing it cool long enough, she smiled. 'Me, too,' she told him softly.

As Isabel passed the burnt shell of the barn on her way to the farmhouse that afternoon, she shuddered. The memory of Ross opening the door and plunging into the smoke and flames was something she would never forget.

Jean must have come home to a nightmare, she thought, and when the farmer's wife opened the door in answer to her knock, there wasn't a vestige of colour in her face. But she was calm, and when she saw who was standing on the doorstep she managed a smile.

'Isabel,' she said in a low voice. 'Do come in. My mother-in-law has gone to pick the children up from school so we won't be disturbed for a while.'

'So what's happening about Brian?' Isabel asked as she seated herself on a high-backed wooden settle.

'They're keeping him in for observation,' Jean said. 'He has some facial burns but they are not too serious, thanks to Dr Templeton. It is his mental state that is causing the most concern. I know what he's like. Brian broods inwardly for a while and then explodes. He doesn't usually mean anything by it, but this time it was different and I feel that I'm to blame for his irrational behaviour. I should never have let him go on thinking that I was going to leave him, but I've been so fed up with his bad temper of late I thought I'd teach him a lesson. If I hadn't been feeling so ill with pneumonia, *my* reasoning might have been more rational, but it wasn't and now we both have to pay the price.

'Something good *has* come out of it, though. My mother-in-law is not without money and she's offered to pay for the rebuilding of the barn and maybe go into partnership with Brian when he is well enough to discuss it, which would take away a lot of the anxiety, money-wise, that he's been experiencing of late.

'I've been to see him this morning and he can't believe that he did what he did. But he will when he comes home and sees what's left of the barn. The police have been to talk to me and have questioned him at the hospital.'

'They've been to the surgery too,' Isabel told her. 'Dr Templeton and I played it down as much as we could for all your sakes, but we had to tell the truth.'

Jean shook her head wearily. 'There are times when I wish we'd never come to this place, but it was what we both wanted and we're not giving up, especially now that Brian's mother is willing to help us. She would have offered before if she'd known that money was tight, but that husband of mine is so independent it just isn't true.'

As she set off back down the winding road that led to the village, Isabel caught sight of Millie walking her dog and she stopped and asked if the retired GP wanted a lift.

'I wouldn't say no,' Millie told her. 'Scamp and I have been out most of the afternoon and my feet are letting me know it.'

When she'd settled the dog in the back and seated herself in the front passenger seat, she said, 'Your father is happier than he's been in a long time, Isabel.'

'You mean because he's moved into the new apartment?' she said.

'Well, yes. That *is* part of it,' Millie replied. 'But something is pleasing him more than that.'

'I can't imagine what that could be,' Isabel said dryly. 'Unless it's because he doesn't have to make out prescriptions or sound chests any more.'

Ignoring the irony, Millie went on, 'It's because Ross and you are getting on so well. Have you ever wondered why he persuaded him to come back to take over the practice?'

This was leading somewhere, Isabel was thinking, but she didn't know where.

'I was under the impression it was because he wanted someone in charge that he could trust, and I hadn't had the experience,' she said cautiously.

'That was part of it,' Millie agreed, 'but the main reason was because of his concern for you.'

'Me!' Isabel spluttered. 'That makes a first! But why was he concerned about me?'

'He was concerned because you'd never had a relationship with a man since Ross left, and in latter years he has begun to feel that he might have made a big mistake in separating you from him like he did. Though at the time he did think it was for the best.'

This was the final humiliation, Isabel thought as anger swept over her in a hot tide. What arrogance on her father's part to think that he could separate them and then reunite them when it suited him—and for the most degrading of reasons, as far as she was concerned.

She was on the shelf and he'd decided to try and foist her off onto Ross by offering him the practice, in the hope that the close contact of working together would do the trick.

Her face was burning with the shame of it. Did Ross know what her father had been planning? she wondered. Did he think that she saw him as her last hope? She cringed at the thought.

By the time they reached Millie's apartment the elderly GP had realised that she'd put her foot in it, and when Isabel stopped the car she said hesitantly, 'Shall we let what I've told you be our little secret?'

'And let my father think that he's still in control of my life?' she flared. 'There was I, thinking that at last I was my own person, free of his bullying ways, and now I find that his latest ploy is trying to marry me off to the very man that he once couldn't wait to see the back of. Does Ross know that he's been picked as the fall guy?'

'I have no idea,' Millie said uneasily. 'I wouldn't have thought so, but he is nobody's fool.'

'True,' Isabel agreed as her anger turned to ice. 'It would seem that the only fool around these parts is me!'

CHAPTER NINE

DISMAY and disappointment were choking her as Isabel put her key in the lock of the front door of the cottage. Once again she was being made to look stupid, she thought miserably as tears welled up.

She was still cringing from what Millie had told her, and knew that if she was to rescue her self-respect she had to avoid Ross as much as possible in future if it wasn't too late. Perhaps she'd let him see that she still loved him. If that *was* the case, what was she going to do about it?

Well, for starters she wasn't going to dine with him tonight, or any other night for that matter. From now on her feelings were going to be so much under control that neither he nor her father would have an inkling of what was going on in her mind.

Should she leave the practice? No, she decided angrily. Though it would serve her father right if she did. But she was made of stronger stuff than that. She loved this place and no one was going to drive her out of it. Somehow she would cope with working with Ross in the practice, but that would be their only contact.

He was no fool. It must have occurred to him when

he'd come back and found her unloved and unwed that she might be willing to stoke up the dead embers. But if he had any inkling that her father was pulling *his* strings as well as hers, what would he have to say about that?

Ross was nobody's fool and she decided grimly that neither was she. Her pride wouldn't let her be. But she was sobbing her heart out as she fed Tess and Puss-Puss.

She looked across at the sink and remembered how she'd told Ross she had to wash her breakfast pots, as well as feeding the only two beings who loved her. Well, the pots could wait. Before she did anything else she was going to cancel their date for the evening before he rang her doorbell and smiled his quizzical smile when she opened the door.

She had already decided what she was going to say to him and she hoped that she wouldn't choke on it with so much misery inside her.

'Hi,' he said easily when he answered the phone. 'If you're ringing to tell me that you've done your chores, I'm afraid that you're ahead of me. I'm busy clearing up after the decorator.'

'No, that isn't why I'm ringing,' she said flatly. 'I've been having a think while I've been doing my rounds and I've decided that I won't be going out with you this evening. I don't think it's a good idea, us being together out of surgery hours. I need my space, Ross.'

There was silence for a moment, then he said in slow puzzlement, 'This is a sudden change of mind. What has brought it on?'

'Nothing,' she told him, trying to keep her voice steady. 'It is just that I was under my father's thumb for so long that I place great value on my freedom.'

'What has that got to do with me?' he asked in the same puzzled tone. 'Please, don't class me with that old control freak.'

'I'm not,' she said. 'I would feel like that with anybody.'

It was a lie. He was the only person in the whole world she'd ever cared about, except for her long-dead mother, and she couldn't bear for him to feel sorry for her, or be dubious about her motives every time she smiled at him.

'I'm coming over,' he said purposefully.

'You'll be wasting your time,' she told him. 'I won't be here.'

'Where will you be?'

'I might go to the cinema.'

'Rather than dine with me?'

'It's like I said, Ross, I need the space.'

'Fine,' he said abruptly. 'You shall have it!' And rang off.

What had all that been about? he wondered irritably as he finished clearing up. All right, Izzy hadn't exactly been turning somersaults at the thought of spending the evening with him, yet he'd known that underneath she had been looking forward to it. There'd been a sparkle in those beautiful eyes of hers.

But something had put her off and he would like to know what. He didn't think it would have anything to do with her father as Paul had kept a low profile since retiring. But he *was* the most likely candidate when it came to upsetting Izzy.

Maybe she was afraid of getting involved with him again. Wary of being hurt a second time. 'I need my space,' she'd said, which made it crystal clear that she didn't want him in her life except during working hours.

When they met up at the surgery the following morning Ross was frostily polite and Isabel wondered dismally if she would be able to keep up the hands-off approach that she'd adopted.

She knew that she owed him a proper explanation, but if she tried the words would stick in her throat. How could she tell him she'd discovered that her father had persuaded him to come back to the village so that he could marry her off to him?

Fortunately Ross had a mind of his own, which would prevent him from being manipulated, but it was how *she* would feel if he ever discovered what Paul had in mind. It would be extreme humiliation all over again and she wasn't going to leave herself wide open to that!

The atmosphere that morning set the temperature for the days to come, with the thought of leaving the practice becoming more frequent, but Isabel told herself stubbornly that it was here that she belonged and here that she was going to stay.

Her father hadn't put in an appearance since Millie had spilt the beans, so Isabel assumed his companion hadn't told him what she'd done, and there was no way that *she* was going to bring it out into the open. But she promised herself that one day she would have it out with him at a time when Ross wasn't around.

The latest news from the Derwents was that Brian would not have to face charges relating to setting fire to the barn. The hospital wasn't dragging its feet either.

A psychiatrist had seen him the day after the fire and had recommended that he be discharged once his chest and lungs were clear of smoke inhalation. He would then be passed on to a community mental health unit where he would receive structured counselling from psychiatric nurses.

'I'll put up with anything,' he told Isabel when she called round one afternoon. 'All that matters is that Jean isn't going to leave me, and with a bit of financial help from my mother, who has been very supportive, I can see the way ahead more clearly.

'You know that I've been to the surgery to thank Dr Templeton for saving my life...and my sanity,' he said as she was leaving, and she nodded.

She *hadn't* known that he'd been to see Ross, but wasn't going to explain to Brian that they only communicated when necessary at the surgery these days. Chit-chat was not on the menu.

Until the day when he was waiting to hear from Jake's parents if the boy was going to be considered for the polymer implant in his jaw area. It had been his suggestion in the first place and the couple, who'd had no idea that such a thing existed, had immediately begun to follow it up.

They were seeing the consultant that day and would hopefully come away with a decision as to whether the boy was to be considered for the amazing new implant that would make such a difference to his life.

Although he hadn't discussed Jake's case with her of late, Isabel knew that Ross was as anxious as his parents that the child should have it done, and if they should be disappointed for any reason he would feel guilty for raising their hopes.

If things had been as they had before she'd discovered that her father wanted to marry her off to Ross, she would have discussed it with Ross at length in a supportive manner, but those days were gone. If they became any more aloof with each other, she could see them ending up writing notes.

The curves that he had described so eloquently that day were disappearing as she was eating very little, and the eyes that were one of her most redeeming features were dull and lifeless as Isabel stuck to the vow that she'd made after talking to Millie.

They hadn't met since. Isabel suspected that the other woman was avoiding her, and not without cause. Yet in a strange sort of way she was grateful to her. Isabel knew that Millie doted on her father. Why, she would never know. But if he was happy, so was she. So much so that she hadn't been able to resist letting his daughter know that for once something pleased him, and in the telling of it Millie had saved her from making a complete fool of herself.

As the day wore on and Ross was still looking grave, Isabel knew that she was weakening. She *should* be supporting him, she told herself. She loved the man. The things that hurt him hurt her, and now their work in the practice was the only thing they had. It was mean-spirited not to be there for him if he needed her, so, instead of one of the receptionists taking him a cup of tea in the middle of the afternoon, she took it in to him.

'Wow!' he said with a brightening of his expression. 'Am I back in favour or something? Are you sure that I'm not invading your space?'

'If you're going to be sarcastic, I'll go,' she said

stiffly. "I'm here because I know that Jake's parents said they would phone you once they'd got the verdict, and you must be on pins.'

'Yes, I am,' he said sombrely. 'It's times like this that make one realise the important things in life. That petty differences and estrangements come a poor second compared to a child with a serious deformity.'

'So you think I'm petty,' she said quietly. 'I don't blame you. All I can say is that I have my reasons for staying away from you, Ross.'

'Tell me what they are. I thought that at least we were friends.'

'Have I ever said that we weren't?'

'Actions often speak louder than words.'

'I'm sorry if I've hurt your feelings.'

'What do *you* know about my feelings, Izzy?'

'Nothing, I suppose,' she told him flatly, and prayed that if *she* were to ask *him* the same question, his answer would be the same. If Ross ever found out that she still loved him, she would want to curl up and die. He was the one. The only one. And if she couldn't have him she would have no one else. There had been other men in her life, but only briefly. Her disinterested attitude had always rung the death knell on any budding relationship.

At that moment the phone rang and as he listened to the voice at the other end he was smiling. 'It's sorted, Izzy,' he said after he'd hung up. 'Jake is going to get the implant. Where it will be done isn't clear yet, with the two countries being involved, but he's on the list and they've been promised as little delay as possible.'

She smiled back at him. In this rare moment of togetherness she was telling herself that she was committing herself to heartbreak because of pride. Why didn't she come right out with it and tell Ross that she loved him?

'That's good news,' she said briskly as she heeded the voice of reason. 'You'll feel better now.' And then returned to her room.

The days were still crawling by and the golden summer of Ross's return was drawing to a close. There were times when Isabel sat in her garden in the evenings with Tess and Puss-Puss beside her, watching the glory of the sunset above the peaks, with a raw craving inside her to be with Ross.

But always at the back of her mind was the fear of rejection. She'd known it twice already in different forms. Her father's rejection of her because she *was* there and her mother wasn't, and the rejection she'd felt when Ross had gone away.

Though she'd discovered since that he would never have left the village if it hadn't been for her father's threats and his concern for her. But that was all it *had* been—concern, not love—and there had been no indication that anything had changed with regard to *his* feelings.

It was on one such evening when she was longing to be with him that her wish was granted. She looked up and he was there, his hand on the latch of the gate that separated the cottage garden from the riverbank. In the fading light his face looked grey and gaunt, and Isabel got slowly to her feet.

'What is it?' she asked as he pushed back the gate and came towards her.

'My mother died an hour ago,' he said in a voice thick with shock and grief.

'Oh, no!' she breathed. 'Not Sally!'

'I'm afraid so.'

'Come here,' she said gently, opening her arms wide, and as if there was no other place he would ever want to be, he stepped into her embrace and cried out his sorrow.

'What happened?' she asked when the tears stopped and he looked down at her with red-rimmed eyes. Taking his hand, she led him into the cottage, and when he'd lowered himself onto the sofa in her small sitting room he said, 'Sophie rang me to say that she'd found Mum on the floor in their bedroom and that she thought she'd had a stroke. I told her to ring for an ambulance and was round there faster than the speed of light, but it was too late. She'd gone, without us being able to say goodbye, or me being able to tell her how much I loved her.'

'Sally would have known that without you telling her,' Isabel said. 'She wouldn't have forgotten how you came back to be near her.'

'Yes. But I came back for other reasons as well.'

''How long since she had her blood pressure checked?'

'A week ago, by me, and it was fine then, though we all know that it could go sky high at the drop of a hat. But she was on medication and had her own means of testing it daily if she wanted to.'

He was getting to his feet.

'I must go, Izzy,' he said reluctantly. 'There are things to be done, arrangements to be made. Obviously I'm not going to sign the death certificate, not for my own mother. You'll need to sign it, and then I'll ask Jim Danvers from the practice in the next village to give us his signature.'

He touched her cheek gently. 'Thanks for being there for me, Izzy. I'm sorry if I invaded your space.'

'Don't say that!' she cried. 'I wish I'd never used that phrase. It's pompous and trite. I only said it because I was afraid of making a fool of myself again.'

He managed a watery smile. 'On this blackest of days you have just brought light into my darkness. Goodnight, Izzy. I'll see you some time tomorrow, I'm not sure when.'

She stood by the window and watched him go, with head erect and a firmer step than when he'd arrived, and though it was a very sad day there was a warm feeling around her heart. Could it be hope? she wondered.

In the week that followed Isabel didn't see much of Ross. With funeral arrangements to see to, his mother's affairs *and* the business of the practice, he had little time to spare. Yet she was hoping that he would say something to keep her hopes alive. But it was as if he had forgotten what he'd said that night at the cottage.

Maybe when he'd said that she'd brought light into the darkness of his mother's death, he'd just been over-emotional, she thought, and it had had nothing to do with her telling him why she'd been staying away from him. But she *had* started to hope that *he* might care for *her* as much as she cared for him. After all, she was the one that he'd come to in his grief, though that might have been because he wasn't well blessed with relations. There was only Sophie, and she would have had her own grief to cope with. As for friends, Ross hadn't been back long enough to make many of those, whereas she knew lots of people around the village.

He did pop into her room on the second day after his mother's death and surprised her by announcing, 'I know that it goes without saying you'll be at the funeral, Izzy, and if you are agreeable I'd like you to be in the first car with Sophie and myself.'

'Me!' she exclaimed. 'But I'm not a relation.'

He had taken her by surprise and in the first moment after he'd asked she'd felt blessed that he wanted her with him, but following quickly on that thought was a vision of her father with a self-satisfied smile on his face when he saw her in the family car. Paul would think that his scheming had paid off. That he'd got her off his hands at last.

Ross was waiting for an answer and she could tell he sensed her hesitation. 'If you're rather not, you have only to say so,' he said levelly.

If she said no, that she would rather travel to the cemetery with the rest of the mourners, she would be denying Ross her support, and herself some moments of closeness with him. That mattered much more than her father thinking how clever he was, so she said evenly, 'It means a lot to me that you've asked me to be with you. Of course I'll do what you ask.'

He smiled.

'Good.'

It wasn't the moment to tell her that he'd found a scrawled note on the arm of his mother's chair, which she must have written as she'd felt the beginning of the end. It was barely decipherable, but he'd managed to make it out. It was made up of just four words. Ross, Follow Your Heart it said, and one day soon he intended to do just that. But he couldn't concentrate on his love for the living until he'd buried the dead that he'd also loved.

* * *

It was late Saturday afternoon and the funeral was over. Almost everyone from the village had been there, and anyone who wanted to had been invited back to the tea-room for refreshments.

Sophie, resplendent in mourning black, was in charge and telling everyone who asked that she was going to carry on as before, with some outside help. 'It's what our Sally would have wanted,' she said. 'She was the brains and I'm the brawn, which is perhaps as well under the circumstances.'

She'd collared Ross one afternoon after his mother's death and told him in her usual forthright manner, 'I saw that note your mother left. Are you going to act on it?'

He'd managed a smile.

'Maybe. You'll have to wait and see, Aunt Sophie.'

Of course he was going to act upon it, he'd thought. He'd already made up his mind on that, but he could wait a few more days until his mother had been laid to rest. He'd waited seven years and now that the time had come he was going to make sure that the setting and the moment were perfect. He hadn't forgotten Sophie telling him about the Kissing Stone and it had caught his imagination.

The three of them had sat in silence in the funeral car, with Ross gazing sombrely ahead and Sophie mopping her eyes. Isabel had ached for them both.

Her father and Millie had been amongst the mourners and she hadn't missed his satisfied smile when he'd seen her seated beside Ross in the family's funeral car. Neither had she been unaware of his companion's sliding glance every time their eyes had met.

It had been the first time she'd seen him since she'd met Millie that day on the hill road, and no doubt the older woman would be hoping that nothing would be said today.

She could rest easy on that, Isabel thought dryly. There was no way she would cross swords with her father on such an occasion. All she was concerned about was Ross.

She'd been too young to remember what it had been like after her mother's funeral, but almost everyone who'd had a death in the family said that it was coping with the awful gap that it had left in their lives once the funeral was over that was the worst.

Ross had come to her for comfort once, but had it just been a spontaneous turning towards the person who was nearest? she kept wondering. Would he let her be there for him again when he was down and suffering? Only Ross knew the answer to that.

The last of those who'd come to pay their respects to Sally had gone, and Sophie for once had given in to exhaustion and gone to have a rest, leaving the two doctors to tidy up the tearooms.

It was history repeating itself, Isabel thought, the two of them clearing up after a gathering in this place, but the reasons were very different. The first time it had been a happy occasion, Ross's homecoming. Today it had been a sad departure they had all turned out for.

'What have you planned for tomorrow?' he asked casually as he dried the last pot.

'Nothing of interest,' she replied. 'Why?'

'I just wondered. We've both had a heavy week. Me with the funeral to arrange, and you being lumbered with some of my surgery duties on top of your own.'

'Surely you don't think I minded.'

'No, Izzy. I'm sure you didn't. You've been great from the start. But I think we should both put our feet up tomorrow. I'm going to have a lie-in and then spend the afternoon sorting out some of my mother's papers.'

'I'll probably catch up on some housework,' she said flatly, having got the message that her usefulness was diminishing. 'And now, if you don't mind, I'll be off. Once again it's feeding time for my animals.'

'Sure,' he said easily. 'I'll see you on Monday.'

Did you really expect anything else? Isabel asked herself as she walked the short distance to the cottage. What did you think Ross was going to do? Sweep away all your doubts and confusions on the very day that he's buried his mother—or on any other day for that matter.

It was a shame to tease her, Ross thought as he watched her go, but he'd needed to find out if she would be at home the following day. It appeared that she would.

After a restless night Isabel awoke feeling sluggish and heavy-eyed, and instead of getting out of bed lay gazing at the rafters above her head. The day stretched ahead endlessly and she was loth for it to begin. Her life was running true to form, she thought. She'd let herself hope that Ross saw her as she was now, cool and confident, yet at the same time desirable, but it looked like a vain hope.

The phone on the bedside table rang, breaking into her thoughts. She picked it up eagerly, hoping that it might be Ross. But it was a strange voice speaking in her ear and what it had to say had her leaping out of bed and flinging on jeans and a thick sweater before she went to rummage in the cupboard beneath the stairs.

Ross was smiling as he approached Isabel's cottage in the early afternoon. He was about to act upon what had been his mother's last message to him, and he hoped that somewhere she would be approving.

He'd spent the morning on the phone to a certain restaurant and persuading Sam Shuttleworth's daughter, the florist, to open up to make him a bouquet of her most beautiful flowers.

She'd eyed him curiously, thinking that only a few days before he'd been in to order a funeral arrangement and now here he was asking for the next thing to a bridal bouquet.

In spite of the week he'd had, Ross had found time to go to a jeweller's in the town, and the ring he was going to put on Izzy's finger lay snugly in a small velvet box in his pocket.

Was he presuming too much? he wondered as he lifted the heavy brass knocker on her old oak door. He would soon know, and if he was wrong and she didn't want him when he asked her to marry him, he would keep on asking until she said she did.

There was no answer and he knocked again, not unduly perturbed. He could hear Tess barking somewhere inside and knew that would bring her to the door. But it didn't and he knocked again and again.

Disappointment washed over him. She'd said she would be in, he thought dismally, and she wasn't, which just served him right for not telling her he was coming round. So much for the big surprise.

A tractor was trundling along the lane, driven by the farmer whose cow had been tucking into Izzy's front lawn early one morning, and Ross waved him down.

'Have you seen anything of Dr West today?' he asked him.

'Aye, briefly,' he said, 'but it's a bit ago. She was pulling out onto the road as I went past and looked as if she wasn't intending wasting any time.'

'I see,' Russ said flatly, accepting that he would have to come back when Izzy returned from wherever she'd gone. The next time he came he would phone first to make sure that it wasn't a wasted journey. But each time he phoned there was no answer and he thought exasperatedly that she was making a day of it.

In the late evening, after trying once more and still getting no answer, he went across to the tea shop to check that all was well with Sophie. She'd rallied from the day before and was doing her usual evening bake for Monday.

'Have you seen anything of Izzy today?' he asked.

She shook her head.

'No. Why?'

'I'm told that she went out early this morning and she still isn't back.'

'She's a big girl now,' his aunt said laughingly. 'She doesn't have to report to you when she goes anywhere, does she?'

'No, of course not,' he said absently. 'But I have a strong feeling of unease, though I don't know why.'

Sophie's hands became still in the flour.

'I think I know where she might be. I don't know why it didn't occur to me before. Jess came round for a cup of tea this morning and said that the cave rescue people have been called out to a serious incident at one of the caves near Castleton. They're all volunteers and Isabel is one of them. The police know they can call on her if a doctor is needed, which is often the case.'

'Which cave?' he asked tersely.

'She didn't say. There are dozens of them in the area.'

'And just how dangerous is it?' Ross asked, with a sick feeling in the pit of his stomach.

'What? The caving or the rescue?'

'Both.'

'The caving is very dangerous if those taking part are untrained and careless, and rescuing them can be even more perilous. It all depends on how badly hurt the caver is and whether there is any risk of flooding or boulder chokes and suchlike.'

He was already disappearing through the tea-shop doorway and calling over his shoulder, 'If she shows up, ask her to stay put until I get back. I'm going to Castleton.'

There'd been nothing to indicate that was where Izzy had gone, he thought as he drove towards the place that housed one of the most famous caves in the area, but from what Sophie had said it seemed there was every likelihood that she'd been called out.

There was just one word beating into his brain as he drove along, DANGEROUS. Izzy must be crazy if she was willing to risk her life for people who had nothing better to do than go crawling around caves, he thought grimly. But maybe she wouldn't be there. Perhaps she'd gone to do some shopping in the town as lots of the stores opened on Sunday.

He could tell he was getting near the cave where the accident had occurred by what was going on around the entrance. It wasn't the famous cavern. It was a lesser-known cave where they were gathered that was having its moment of fame. The police were there and an ambulance, and the press were hovering, avid for a story.

As he surveyed the scene Ross saw Izzy's Mini parked nearby, but there was no sign of its owner.

CHAPTER TEN

Ross parked his car next to Izzy's and was out of it in a flash. 'What's going on here?' he asked a police officer who appeared to be in charge.

'We have two people trapped inside one of the caverns,' he was told. 'In caving language there's been a boulder choke—to the rest of us a rockfall.'

'Who are they?' he asked urgently.

'A young woman doctor and a caver knocked unconscious after he fell over some rubble.'

'Not Dr Isabel West?' he questioned as urgency turned to dread.

The officer was observing him intently. 'Yes,' he said. 'Do you know her?'

'We're doctors in a village practice.'

'So you're a doctor, too. That's good. We might need you.'

'I'll do anything I can to assist,' he told him hoarsely. 'If you want someone to go down there, I'll do it. I'm not a caver but I do have basic rescue training.'

While he'd been speaking it had started to rain, and it wasn't drizzle. It was a heavy downpour and Ross could hear someone saying, 'This could cause a flash flood if it keeps up. There's a stream running through the cavern where they're trapped.'

'So who raised the alarm?' Ross asked the policeman, trying to remain detached.

'His companion left him to come up for help,' the officer said, 'and by the time he'd got to the surface he was in such a state he couldn't face going down again. He must have been blundering around down there and disturbed the loose limestone blocks in the roof.

'The doctor was first on the scene and, cool as a cucumber, she went down on her own, leaving instructions for the cave rescue team to bring a stretcher with them when they go down.'

'I know that particular cavern,' the man who'd mentioned flash flooding said. 'It will be a long tight crawl to reach it and stretchering an injured man out of it won't be easy.'

'So boulders have fallen and blocked off the entrance since Dr West went down?'

'That's about it,' he replied. 'It was probably the other fellow panicking to get out that disturbed them. The experienced caver knows to treat the limestone slabs with respect, but novices like these two go in head first, land themselves in a mess and put other people's lives at risk getting them out. Caving can be a dangerous pastime.'

'So what is being done to get them out?' Ross asked the policeman frantically.

'We're waiting for the main cave rescue team to arrive. They'd been called out to another emergency at a place some miles distant and are on their way. The doctor was the only one available in the first instance. They tell us it could be a good hour before they get here, and if the rain keeps coming down like this she and the injured caver are going to be in a dangerous situation.'

'And what will *they* do when they come that *we* can't?' he cried.

'Find a way through the blockage if there is one.'

'Is there any spare gear knocking about?' Ross asked, desperately aware that the minutes were ticking by.

'Why?' the policeman asked. '*You* can't go down there if you've had no experience of caving.'

'How far in are they?' he persisted.

'According to the fellow who raised the alarm, they're trapped in the second of a series of caverns. This cave goes back a long way.'

The flash-flood man spoke. 'I'm not usually willing to put myself at risk because of amateurs, but that young doctor down there is another matter. They'll let you have some gear from the caving shop over there, and once you're togged up I'll take you down. You'll have to follow my instructions to the letter. All right?'

'Anything you say,' Ross agreed fervently. And after he'd dashed into the shop and galvanised the staff into supplying the necessary equipment, he told the assembled crowd, 'I'm going to marry that woman down there and nothing is going to stop me, so start praying for the rain to stop and the rescue team to get here quickly.'

This was a nightmare, Isabel was thinking. She'd been in this sort of situation before, but not on her own. There had always been the rest of the team working alongside her and she had expected that they wouldn't be far behind her when she'd gone down.

She'd thrown herself on top of the injured caver when slabs from the roof had come crashing down and had narrowly escaped being hit, and now she was watching uneasily for any further movement. To make matters worse, the water in the stream that ran through the centre of the cave was rising, which meant that it was raining above ground.

The man had regained consciousness and was moaning loudly beside her, but there was no way she could move him without help. When the rest of the team arrived they would have to pick their way through the boulders that were blocking the way and there was nothing to say that there wouldn't be another fall while they were doing it. Any experienced caver knew that the slightest vibration or movement could cause boulders to come crashing down if they were in a precarious position.

The man was conscious enough to realise that the water level in the cave was rising and kept crying, 'We're going to drown, aren't we?'

From the light on her headgear Isabel could see that his temple was still bleeding from the fall. It was a deep gash and blood was oozing from beneath the dressing she'd put on it. As for the rest of him, there was no room to examine him further, but she suspected there would be other injuries that as yet weren't identifiable.

She was aware that it wasn't advisable to move someone after a head injury if there was any suspected damage to the skull, but the situation they were in presented no choice.

'There's a ledge just behind us,' she said, her gaze on the rising level of the stream. 'Somehow or other we have to climb onto it. I can't lift you on my own. You'll have to help me move you up there. We are going to have to get you upright while I heave you up. Do you think you can stand?'

'I'll have to, won't I?' he cried. 'But there's something wrong with my ankle. I think it might be broken.'

'It's possible that it is,' she told him. 'But I can't risk taking your boot off in these conditions. So you're going to have to put all your weight on the other foot while I get you up there.'

She was cool, organised as much as she could be in such a situation, but at the back of Isabel's mind was the sickening thought that if the others didn't arrive and get them out of here soon, she would never see Ross again. They would have disappeared into the black, fast-flowing water that would soon be filling the cave.

At last they were on the ledge. With a lot of pulling, pushing and agonised cries every time the man put any pressure on his ankle, she'd got him up there.

A vision of Ross, warm and comfortable in the study he'd made for himself above the surgery, came to mind. He would be going through his mother's papers and tying up any loose ends that her death had left.

He would be thinking that she was busy at the cottage, doing the housework that she'd promised herself, and would be enjoying having some time to himself after the events of recent days. Little did he know that unless someone soon came to their rescue, they were going to drown.

As Ross and the experienced caver eased themselves and a folded stretcher along the narrow tunnel that his guide had warned him of, Ross was thinking grimly that

Izzy had gone this way before them, on her own, with no back-up to assist. She was some woman. But why, oh, why, he thought frantically, did she have to do this at the very time he was going to ask her to marry him?

Would they ever be together in this world? he wondered grimly. He'd told the waiting crowd at the entrance to the cave that he was going to marry her, that nothing was going to stop him, but it had been wild talk. He was a doctor in a country practice, not Superman.

'How much further?' he called to the man at the front end of the stretcher as the claustrophobic nightmare continued.

'Shush,' the man whispered. 'Even voice vibrations can cause rock movement. We're almost there. I can see the rubble ahead of me, about six feet away from the end of the tunnel.'

When they stood on the floor of the cavern it was dry, but they could hear water thundering along at the other side of the boulders and his companion said, 'Thankfully the stream veers away at this point, otherwise it could flood the tunnel.'

Ross was observing the pile of stone in front of them in bleak dismay.

'So they are on the other side of this?'

'Yes, if they've not been swept away. It's no use trying to attract their attention. They won't be able to hear us above the noise of the water.'

Ross nodded grimly. This fellow who was so capable and cool was adding to his fears with every word he spoke. Yet he knew that what he said would be correct. The man had the authority of someone with the experience and knowhow to get them out of this if anybody could.

Why had he waited so long to tell Izzy that he loved her? he thought wretchedly as his mind veered from one desperate thought to another.

'We have to pick our way through this lot,' the caver was saying. 'It won't be easy and it won't be fast.'

'So we're not going to try to move the blockage?'

'Can't risk it. We might bring the whole roof down on us, and them. Follow me and tread carefully.'

As they moved painstakingly across the boulder-strewn floor of the cave, the space for movement was getting less as the piled rubble became higher and Ross couldn't see how they were going to get past it without moving it. But incredibly the man in front had found an opening, a narrow cleft between the stones, and as they squeezed through it they saw a faint chink of light ahead of them.

A few seconds more of careful manoeuvring and they'd squeezed themselves through and could see the swirling dark waters only feet away. Looking down at him in blank astonishment was Izzy.

'Hello, there,' he said as calm descended on him. In that moment it was sufficient to know that she was alive, and if anything did happen to them at least they would be together. He hadn't been at his best on the arduous journey to the cave, but now he was coming into his own as a doctor. Being acutely aware that it was not the moment for a blissful reunion, he switched his glance to the injured man and asked, 'What's the score with our friend here, Izzy?'

'James tripped over the rubble on the floor and knocked himself out. He was unconscious when I got here but breathing satisfactorily. While I was treating his head wound the boulder choke occurred and where I might have been able to find a way out myself, there was no way I could have managed to move him on my own, so we stayed put and hoped that soon someone would appear.'

She'd been calm enough while explaining the circumstances that had brought about this eerie meeting in what had once been an old mine, but her voice broke as she told him, 'I never dreamt that the someone would be you.'

Ross didn't reply. There were a thousand things he wanted to say to her, but not now. He was feeling the man's pulse and shining a torch in his eyes and at the same time watching his companion, weighing up the force of the water that was still mercifully veering away from them.

'Would you say it's still rising?' the experienced caver asked Isabel.

'No,' she told him. 'I've thought a few times in the last quarter of an hour that the water level was beginning to drop, but it's so dark in here I could be wrong.'

He nodded and, turning to Ross, said, 'Let's get the party under way. We've got about three feet of space to get this guy onto the stretcher without any of us falling into the water. Once he's on it I'll take the front end, Dr West can take the back, and you can crawl underneath it for support when we get to tricky corners and suchlike.'

'I'd rather Dr West was at the front,' Ross told him, 'so that she won't be separated from us if there are any more boulder chokes.'

'All right,' he replied tightly, 'but let's get moving, and remember to put your weight on your forearms rather than your wrists. That way you'll do less damage to your hands while you're crawling over rubble.'

The way back, with the stretcher to manipulate, was painfully slow, making the journey inwards seem like child's play. But at last they had climbed through and over the fallen stone and were in the tunnel, moving towards the entrance to the first cavern and from there to safety, with Izzy just a few feet away at the front of the stretcher, grave and silent but alive.

When they appeared at the lighted entrance to the caves a cheer went up and someone in the crowd shouted, 'So when's the wedding, Doc?'

Ross flashed them a muddy smile.

'Soon, I hope!' he said with meaning, and as laughter followed his reply he saw the question in Izzy's eyes. But before he could say anything the police, paramedics, media and the rescue team, who had only recently arrived after their Land Rover had broken down up on the moors, were surrounding them.

When the injured caver had been taken to hospital and the fuss had died down, Ross looked around him for the man who had been there for him during one of the most terrifying experiences of his life, but he was nowhere to be seen and when he asked if anyone knew where he was he drew a blank.

'He was with us when we came out of the cave,' Ross insisted. 'An experienced caver, he knew exactly what he was doing and guided me to Dr West.'

But everyone he asked said that they hadn't seen him. Finally he sought out the policeman he'd talked to when he'd first arrived. '*You* saw me with the man who took me down into the cave, didn't you?' he begged.

'Yes. Why?' he asked.

'I want to thank him for what he did. Without him I would have been useless.'

He nodded. 'The fellow certainly seemed to know what he was doing, but since you all came up to ground level there's a lot going on and I haven't seen him anywhere around. I'll give you a shout if I do, but he might be camera-shy. The press are all over the place and they've been after him, too. You know, hero of the day sort of thing.'

He certainly was that, Ross thought as he turned away and found Isabel by his side, and Izzy, tired and muddied but beautiful to him, had been the heroine of the day. A day that he was never going to forget.

'What's wrong?' she asked.

'I want to thank the fellow who helped us,' he told her, 'but he's disappeared and no one seems to have seen him. If it hadn't been for the police officer remembering him, I might be thinking I imagined him taking me down into the depths. You saw him, didn't you?'

'Yes, of course I did!' she exclaimed. 'He was heaven-sent. Confident, cool and knowledgeable. He's probably gone on his way now that all the panic is over, not wanting any fuss.'

One of the rescue team standing nearby had heard the conversation and said with a smile, 'It sounds as if you've met Jack Benedict. Describe him to me.'

'Sixtyish,' Ross told him. 'Lean and long with grey eyes and a beard. I couldn't see his hair because of his helmet, but he had a scar down the side of his face.'

'That's him,' the man said. 'Jack got the scar from a rockfall some years ago. He used to be in the rescue team with us until he retired a couple of years back, but he still goes caving. It's his life, and there is no one more capable. He's a bit of a recluse and would run a mile if he thought the press were after him.'

'Where can we find him?' Isabel asked.

'I don't know. He has a cottage somewhere high amongst the peaks and if you found it he wouldn't thank you for calling.'

As they observed him uncertainly he smiled. 'He'll know you're grateful, and if you want to show him how much, leave him in peace.'

'*I'm* driving you home,' Ross said when the other man had gone to join the rest of the rescue team. 'We'll pick up *your* car tomorrow.'

When he'd settled Isabel into the passenger seat he tucked a rug around her legs and smiled down at her, but she didn't look up.

'I have questions to ask,' she told him sombrely.

'Fire away then,' he said easily.

'First of all, when are you going to tell me how you happened to be at the caves?'

'I'd been trying to get in touch with you ever since midday,' he explained. 'I went round to the cottage and when you weren't there I kept phoning. Early this evening Sophie told me what was happening in Castleton and, remembering what you'd once said about being involved in cave rescue, I thought you might be there. I was praying that you wouldn't be putting yourself in such danger, but as soon as I arrived I knew it was a vain hope.'

'Why were you trying to get in touch with me?'

Why indeed? he thought. He'd been so full of his plans, with the table booked and the flowers ready for the special moment, and what had happened? He'd ended up in a state of complete horror at the thought of losing the woman he loved, to the extent that he'd gone scrabbling about in the bowels of the earth to find her. And now, thankfully, here she was beside him, asking innocently why he'd called round to see her.

'I came round because there was something I wanted to say to you,' he said gently.

'What was it?'

'The time isn't right, Izzy. I want to get you home so that you can get into a hot bath and have a meal.'

'I'm not hungry.'

'You should be after all that exertion.'

'Something I heard outside the caves took away my appetite.'

'And what was that?'

'Somebody asked you when the wedding was, and you said that you hoped it would be soon. Are you getting married?'

'Maybe. It's not settled yet.'

He watched as a single tear rolled down her cheek and couldn't hold out any longer.

'You are amazing, Izzy,' he said with the same gentleness as he pulled up at the side of the road. 'You went into those caves full of confidence, without giving it a second thought. Yet when it comes to us, you are so unsure of yourself it just isn't true. It is *you* I want to marry. I was coming round today to ask you to be my wife but, unpredictable woman that you are, you weren't there.

'The table I'd booked for tonight will have stood unused, the flowers that Sam Shuttleworth's daughter made up for me this morning will be past their best, but one thing won't have suffered in the process. I checked to make sure when I replaced my jacket after taking off the caving gear.' Putting his hand into his pocket, he pulled out the box that he'd been carrying around all day.

'Will you marry me, Izzy?' he asked softly, lifting the lid to show a solitaire diamond ring. As it sparkled up at her he continued, 'I never realised how much I loved you until I came back to the village and found that the tearful teenager I'd left behind had turned into a dedicated young doctor who made me want to make love to her every time I saw her.'

'Really?' she breathed. 'Are you sure you've got the right person?'

'Very sure, and if we weren't cramped inside the car I would show you just how sure I am. But you haven't given me an answer.'

'I feel as if I've loved you for ever,' she whispered, 'but I never expected *you* to love *me*.'

'Which just goes to show how wrong one can be,' he said laughingly.

'Of course I'll marry you, Ross,' she said chokily. 'Any time you like. But how did those people at the caves know about us?'

'As I was preparing to go down, I told them that I was going to marry you and nothing was going to stop me, so they had better pray that the rain would stop and the rescue team arrive.'

'That was the strangest thing, wasn't it?' she said dreamily, after he'd slid the ring on to her finger. 'That such an experienced caver happened to be in the right place at the right time, and once he'd done his bit he went, not wanting any fuss.'

She straightened up suddenly in the passenger seat and turned towards him, her face full of dismay.

'What is it?' he asked.

'My father!' she exclaimed. 'When he knows we're going to be married, he will think he's still pulling my strings.'

'In that case, I think he should be the first one to know,' Ross suggested, 'so that we can make sure he understands that those days are over.'

'Yes,' she agreed immediately.

They'd showered together at the cottage, kissing, laughing, adoring each other, as a pearly dawn crept over the sky, and now they were seated at the kitchen table, having their first breakfast together.

'Should we be so happy?' Isabel said. 'So soon after you losing your mother?'

Ross smiled.

'Yes. I think so.' He took a crumpled piece of paper out of his pocket and passed it to her. 'That was her last message to me. I think that my mother had always known where my heart lay, maybe before I knew myself, and this is what she wanted for us, Izzy.'

He looked across the table at the sweet, scrubbed cleanliness of her and said softly, 'You have no idea how much I want to make love to you, but I've waited a long time for you, Izzy, and, that being so, I can wait a little longer. Let's set a date for the wedding and then go and get your father up, if he isn't up already.'

Paul *was* up. He didn't sleep much these days. Whether it was due to a guilty conscience or old age, he wasn't sure, but he was well and truly awake when he opened the door to Isabel and Ross.

'You folks are up early,' he said with a dry smile as he stepped back to let them in. 'To what do I owe the honour of a visit from my daughter?'

'We've come to tell you that we are getting married,' Isabel told him without preamble.

'Ah!'

'And to let you know that although you might think you've manipulated us, you haven't. I have always wanted Ross and now have my heart's desire.'

'Yes, of course you have,' her father said calmly. 'That is why I finally admitted to myself that I'd made a mistake separating you from him. That if I hadn't interfered you would probably still have gone to medical school and been a much happier student.

'So I asked him to come back to take over the practice. It was true when I said that I wanted it to go to someone I could trust and Ross was the best GP I had ever worked with. But the main reason was to see if you two really did want each other and now, when the time comes, I will die with my conscience appeased.'

As Isabel observed him goggle-eyed, trying to take in the fact that her father was almost apologising *and* professing to have a conscience into the bargain, Ross spoke for the first time.

'Are you saying that from now on you're going to be the father you should have been to Izzy?'

The dry smile was there again.

'It's a bit late to try to teach an old dog new tricks

but, yes, I'm going to try. I wouldn't want to miss out on my grandchildren like I missed out on my daughter.'

They had finally managed to dine at the restaurant up on the moors and as they'd enjoyed good food and wine Ross had said, 'This is my third attempt to bring you here and I've finally succeeded.'

'It's very nice,' Isabel had told him, 'but why this place especially?'

'I'll show you when we've finished eating,' he'd promised, and had taken her through a moonlit garden to where a big black stone stood.

'It's the Kissing Stone!' she'd exclaimed. 'They say that lovers who kiss while touching it will be together for ever.'

'Exactly,' he'd said as he'd placed their hands side by side on the smooth surface of the stone, and as she'd lifted her mouth for his kiss he'd murmured, 'We already know that nothing will ever separate us, but we couldn't let this old stone not work its magic, could we?'

Once again the Riverside Tea Shop was going to be crowded with village folk. In recent months there'd been a homecoming buffet set out there, then a short time ago a funeral tea, and today it was to be a wedding banquet for the two village doctors.

Isabel West, who most of them had known since she'd been small, and Ross Templeton, Sally's son, who had followed his heart and found the love of his life, were going to make their vows in a packed village church. Flanked by the father of the bride on the one side, and on the other the best man, a farmer from up on the tops called Brian Derwent, who was looking surprisingly happy and content for once.

MILLS & BOON

Medical romance™

presents an exciting and emotional new trilogy from bestselling author Kate Hardy

Posh Docs!

HONOURABLE, ELIGIBLE AND IN DEMAND!

Her Celebrity Surgeon

On sale 6th January 2006

Don't miss the next two novels
Her Honourable Playboy *(on sale 3rd March 2006)*
His Honourable Surgeon *(on sale 5th May 2006)*
– only from Medical Romance!

Available at most branches of WHSmith, Tesco, ASDA, Borders, Eason, Sainsbury's and most bookshops

Visit our website at www.millsandboon.co.uk

MILLS & BOON
Live the emotion

Medical romance™

NEEDED: FULL-TIME FATHER
by Carol Marinelli

The grand opening of Heatherton A&E doesn't quite go to plan, so nurse manager Madison Walsh must rely on, and trust, new consultant Guy Boyd to save the day. Trusting turns to loving, but Madison has her daughter's happiness to consider...

TELL ME YOU LOVE ME *by Gill Sanderson*

John Cameron is a loner, travelling the world as a professional diver. For reasons of his own he's wary of getting close to anyone – until he meets Dr Abbey Fraser. John instinctively knows he needs to be part of her life. Then they discover they share a secret...

THE SURGEON'S ENGAGEMENT WISH
by Alison Roberts

Nurse Beth Dawson has chosen small town life for some peace and quiet. The last person she expects to meet is Luke Savage, the high-flying surgeon she was once engaged to! Luke has changed, mellowed – realised what's important in life. But will he forgive Beth for leaving him?

A&E DRAMA: Pulses are racing in these fast-paced dramatic stories

On sale 3rd February 2006

Available at WHSmith, Tesco, ASDA, Borders, Eason, Sainsbury's and most bookshops

www.millsandboon.co.uk

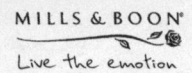

MILLS & BOON®

Live the emotion

Medical
romance™

SHEIKH SURGEON by Meredith Webber

Dr Nell Warren fell madly in love with Sheikh Khalil al Kalada – but he could never be hers. Now Nell must journey to the oasis city where Kal is a successful surgeon. He is the only man who can save her son's life. Not because of his skill – but because he is Patrick's father...

THE DOCTOR'S COURAGEOUS BRIDE
by Dianne Drake

Dr Solange Léandre has dedicated her life to the rural clinic in Kijé island. When specialist Paul Killian visits, he's mesmerised by her. But how can this city doctor show Solange that he has the dedication for life in the jungle – and the passion to care for a strong-willed woman?

24:7 Feel the heat – every hour...every minute... every heartbeat

THE EMERGENCY DOCTOR'S PROPOSAL
by Joanna Neil

Consultant Mark Ballard is challenging and demanding – yet somehow he awakens doctor Sarah Marshall's desires. As they work together, Sarah secretly hopes their professional respect will become personal. When she gets another job offer – from a former lover – it's time for Mark to take a stand!

On sale 3rd February 2006

Available at WHSmith, Tesco, ASDA, Borders, Eason, Sainsbury's and most bookshops

www.millsandboon.co.uk

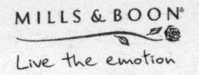

MILLS & BOON®

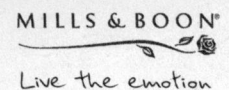

Live the emotion

Millionaire's Mistress

In February 2006, By Request brings back three favourite romances by our bestselling Mills & Boon authors:

The Sicilian's Mistress by Lynne Graham
The Rich Man's Mistress by Cathy Williams
Marriage at His Convenience by Jacqueline Baird

Make sure you buy these passionate stories!

On sale 3rd February 2006

Available at WHSmith, Tesco, ASDA, Borders, Eason, Sainsbury's and most bookshops

www.millsandboon.co.uk

MILLS & BOON®

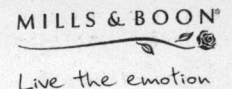

Live the emotion

Bewitched by the Boss

In February 2006, By Request brings back three favourite romances by our bestselling Mills & Boon authors:

The Boss's Virgin by Charlotte Lamb
The Corporate Wife by Leigh Michaels
The Boss's Secret Mistress by Alison Fraser

Make sure you buy these irresistible stories!

On sale 3rd February 2006

Available at WHSmith, Tesco, ASDA, Borders, Eason, Sainsbury's and most bookshops

www.millsandboon.co.uk

BEFORE SUNRISE
by Diana Palmer

Enter a world of passion, intrigue and heartfelt emotion. As two friends delve deeper into a murder investigation they find themselves entangled in a web of conspiracy, deception...and a love more powerful than anything they've ever known.

THE BAY AT MIDNIGHT
by Diane Chamberlain

Her family's cottage on the New Jersey shore was a place of freedom and innocence for Julie Bauer – until tragedy struck...

Don't miss this special collection of original romance titles by bestselling authors.

Available at WH Smith, Tesco, ASDA, Borders, Eason, Sainsbury's and all good paperback bookshops

www.millsandboon.co.uk

LAKESIDE COTTAGE
by Susan Wiggs

Each summer Kate Livingston returns to her family's lakeside cottage, a place of simple living and happy times. But her quiet life is shaken up by the arrival of an intriguing new neighbour, JD Harris…

50 HARBOUR STREET
by Debbie Macomber

Welcome to the captivating world of Cedar Cove, the small waterfront town that's home to families, lovers and strangers whose day-to-day lives constantly and poignantly intersect.

Don't miss this special collection of original romance titles by bestselling authors.

Available at WH Smith, Tesco, ASDA, Borders, Eason, Sainsbury's and all good paperback bookshops

www.millsandboon.co.uk

M&B

4 FREE

BOOKS AND A SURPRISE GIFT!

We would like to take this opportunity to thank you for reading this Mills & Boon® book by offering you the chance to take FOUR more specially selected titles from the Medical Romance™ series absolutely FREE! We're also making this offer to introduce you to the benefits of the Reader Service™—

- ★ FREE home delivery
- ★ FREE gifts and competitions
- ★ FREE monthly Newsletter
- ★ Exclusive Reader Service offers
- ★ Books available before they're in the shops

Accepting these FREE books and gift places you under no obligation to buy, you may cancel at any time, even after receiving your free shipment. Simply complete your details below and return the entire page to the address below. You don't even need a stamp!

YES! Please send me 4 free Medical Romance books and a surprise gift. I understand that unless you hear from me, I will receive 6 superb new titles every month for just £2.75 each, postage and packing free. I am under no obligation to purchase any books and may cancel my subscription at any time. The free books and gift will be mine to keep in any case.

M6ZED

Ms/Mrs/Miss/Mr .... Initials ....

BLOCK CAPITALS PLEASE

Surname ....

Address ....

....

.... Postcode ....

Send this whole page to:
UK: FREEPOST CN81, Croydon, CR9 3WZ

Offer valid in UK only and is not available to current Reader service subscribers to this series. Overseas and Eire please write for details. We reserve the right to refuse an application and applicants must be aged 18 years or over. Only one application per household. Terms and prices subject to change without notice. Offer expires 30th April 2006. As a result of this application, you may receive offers from Harlequin Mills & Boon and other carefully selected companies. If you would prefer not to share in this opportunity please write to The Data Manager, PO Box 676, Richmond, TW9 IWU.

Mills & Boon® is a registered trademark owned by Harlequin Mills & Boon Limited.
Medical Romance™ is being used as a trademark. The Reader Service™ is being used as a trademark.